THE ROYAL ACADEMY

NYT & USA TODAY BESTSELLING AUTHOR

JESSICA SORENSEN

THE ROYAL ACADEMY

THE ROYAL ACADEMY
BOOK 1

JESSICA SORENSEN

 Created with Vellum

ONE
MADDISON

Walking this late at night might not have been one of my brightest ideas, but I don't have a choice, either. A lot of my ideas aren't great, but this one is definitely turning out to be an epic mistake.

The moon is nonexistent tonight, thanks to the heavy overcast of pollution. Between that, the fact that over half the lampposts that line the littered street are burned out, and even more of the nearby houses and shops are boarded up, the area is smothered in darkness.

Plenty of people are roaming around, but that makes me even more uneasy, since most of them are dealers or gang members.

"Hey, baby, what're you doing out so late by yourself?" A guy about ten years older than me creeps out from the shadows of a nearby alley. He's wearing holey jeans, a stained white shirt, and he's carrying a brown paper bag that's for sure hiding a bottle of alcohol.

I bite back the snarky comment burning at the tip of my tongue. *Do not get into a fight this late, Maddy. It's not worth it.*

I keep repeating the mantra as I quicken my pace while wrapping my arms around myself. I'm wearing shorts and a gray T-shirt, my wavy long brown hair is pulled back into a ponytail, and the thick soles of my boots scuff against the sidewalk that's covered in trash. That's typical for the northside of Royal City. But the southside of the city matches the name—the towering buildings and homes that are all splashed with wealth, glitter, and glam. Not the northside, though. No, the northside is polluted, grimy, and constantly smells like fish due to the canal that runs parallel to the area. When I was younger, I used to go down there and walk along it, pretending that it was a river in the mountains. I had a wicked imagination back then, but life has worn me down big time.

"Aw, come on." The man stumbles after me, either intoxicated and/or high "Don't be shy. I was just asking you a question."

Irritation bursts inside, and I snap, "Go to hell," from over my shoulder. Then I wince.

Shit. I probably made things worse.

Why do I have to open my mouth? Because I'm stupid? Repressed? Have spent years bottling up my rage?

Maybe a little bit of all three.

I pat my pocket for my pepper spray then realize I forgot it back at work. It's sitting in my cubby with my apron. Dammit!

"Is that an invitation?" the man slurs.

I pick up my pace to a jog, and he laughs.

"Hey, come back! I'm not done playin' with you!"

I run. Normally, I can run much faster than I can now. In fact, I've won a lot of medals for the track and cross country team. However, I wasn't wearing thick, heavy boots when I did that. That leaves my speed limited, although I can still move pretty fast.

It's a bold move to run in this particular part of the town where blending in and not drawing attention is a necessity for survival. But I'm not about to let Dumbass Drunk Man catch up with me. Sure, he's wasted, and I might be able to hold my own if I have to fight him off. I'd rather avoid the violence, though, for a lot of reasons, one being that I'm already on probation due to an incident where I hit a man after he smacked my ass when I walked by. I got the blame, of course, which is totally unfair and probably seems crazy. But the man who smacked my ass was also the vice principal of my high school that I graduated from three months ago. No one believed my side of the story. Why would they when the vice principal is friends with the governor of the city and other powerful politicians? And me? I'm just trailer trash from the northside of the city. And my mom's a drunk, and my father's in prison.

I was lucky just to get put on probation. And so far, it hasn't been too big of a deal, but if the police have to show up now because I'm in a fight, I could get blamed for it. Then I might get jail time since I'm eighteen now.

Freakin' adult responsibilities suck big time, but I'll handle them as maturely as possible—

I slam into something rock solid and stumble back, crossing my fingers it's a wall. When I glance up, however, the worst-case scenario is standing before me.

His name Drew, but everyone calls him Scar Man—and yeah, the guy is as dumb as his name. He declared the title himself, too, after he got a scar on his lip. A scar that he got when he tripped over his own shoelaces and ended up falling and smacking his face on the curb. But when people ask him, he tells them he got hit in the face by a mob boss.

I know the truth because I grew up with him and can remember when he fell. We used to be friends, too—sort of—but that ended when he started dealing and I wanted no part of it. My father's a dealer, and now he's behind bars. I have no dreams of following in his footsteps. I'm going to college in just a couple of days. I wish I could've gone to a university somewhere far away from here, but I can't afford it. Thankfully, due to my academic and athletic success, I was able to get a scholarship at Royal City Community College. Once I graduate from there, I'm moving so far away from here and never looking back

"Maddy," Drew—yeah, I refuse to call him Scar Man—greets me with a smirk.

"Drew," I reply like I'm bored when, in all actuality, I'm on edge.

Drew runs with a group of people who despise my father because he narced on them when he got arrested in exchange for a lighter sentence. Since the people that he got arrested can't get to him, they use their lackeys out here to try to use me as their punching bag. This is part of the reason why I shouldn't have been roaming around town this late at night. But I had to work the night shift at the diner I've been employed at for two years. Usually, I request not to work late, but it pays time and a half, and the boss needed me to fill in for someone. Plus, tips are better during the later hours, since most of the patrons are drunk. I need the money because the scholarship doesn't cover books and other expenses. Just tuition.

Drew's lips twitch. "I told you not to call me that anymore. It's Scar Man."

I roll my eyes. "Dude, I hate to break it to you, but Scar Man is a stupid name."

His fingers curl into fists. He's a massive guy that rolls in at about six-four and weighs about two hundred and forty pounds. While I highly doubt he'll hit me, a tiny bit of doubt causes me to spin around and run.

"Maddy!" he calls after me. "Don't run! You'll only make it worse!"

I've been avoiding Drew since my dad outed his gang of friends and got half of them arrested. I knew once I ran into one of them, I'd probably get dragged down an alleyway and get my butt beat. And that's the best-case scenario. The worse is that I'll end up in the smelly canal with northside's discarded trash and the people that overdose.

I take off into a full-on sprint, heading in the wrong direction of my house, meaning I'll have to backtrack. I round back around the corner, only to find that the drunk guy from earlier is still lurking nearby. When he spots me, he gives me a huge, yellow-teeth grin.

"You're back." He flicks his cigarette onto the ground then stumbles toward me.

Cursing under my breath, I hurry across the street. But halfway across, I slam to a halt at the sight of three of Drew's friends heading toward me. I reel back around, but Drew is right there.

His arms circle around me. "Just stop fighting it, Maddy. You know you're going to have to pay his debt sooner or later, so just get it over with."

"Never!" I try to slam my head against his face, but Drew manages to dodge it. Then, using his strength, he pins me against him as the other people reach us.

Elli, who's the tallest and bulkiest of the bunch, stops right in front of me. "I'd like to pass along a message to your father, Maddy," he tells me with a grin. "He will pay his debt when he gets out of jail. And if he doesn't, his punishment will be worse than the one you're about to get."

I try to wiggle my way out of Drew's grip, but he's way too strong. "I don't even talk to my father," I insist. "I hate him more than you guys do."

Elli lets out a hollow laugh. "Your father is the reason my brother's in jail and why my mama started drinking again, so trust me when I say that's bullshit."

Now I'm the one to hollowly laugh. "Yeah, well, my father beat me and my mother for eighteen years, so eat shit, Elli."

His lips twitch in annoyance, and then he slips on brass

knuckles. "I don't give a shit about you or your mother. You father's debt needs to be paid, and either your mother or you are going to do it for him."

While I'm not a fan of my mother, I don't hate her; I just pity her. She's been married to my abusive father for twenty-plus years. It's a sad, tragic life that I've tried to convince her to leave, yet she always stands by him.

But I'm not about to stand here and let this guy beat me up. I'm a fighter. I had to be since the day I came into this world kicking and screaming. According to stories my grandma used to tell before she died, I was the loudest, angriest baby she'd ever seen. I don't think I was angry, though. I think I somehow knew what was waiting for me in the future and was absolutely terrified.

I push up on my feet, lift up, and slam my boots into Elli's face, hitting him right in the nose. He cries out in pain, and Drew lets out a string of curses, his grip around me loosening. I seize the opportunity to elbow him in the gut. He grunts, hunching over and letting me go. Then I swing right and run down the road.

"Get her!" someone shouts.

Footsteps hammer after me.

I run as fast as I can, which is pretty damn fast, for about thirty seconds, and it feels like I have a chance of getting away. But then red and blue lights illuminate the street. A split-second later, three police vehicles are blocking my way. I'd be relieved, but my past experiences with police haven't been fantastic.

My worry becomes justified when an officer gets out of his

car and yells, "Stop right where you are, Maddison, and put your hands up."

Great. I know the officer. He's the one who arrested me the last time and who seems to be besties with my vice principal. Plus, he loathes my dad.

Dammit, I'm screwed.

All jails smell the same, like urine and body odor, but with an over-masking scent of pungent lemon air freshener. Someone is usually coughing, too, either because they're sick or they smoke too much—it could be either or.

My dad used to get arrested frequently, for all sorts of various things, like public intoxication, assault, and drug possession. My mother would bail him out, and he rarely got much jail time. However, three months ago, when he was arrested, he apparently had enough drugs on him that police were able to give him a trafficking charge. My father insisted he was being set up, and my mother wasted what little money we had on a lawyer for him. It didn't work, and the only thing he could do to not spend a long time in jail was narc.

"What're you in here for? Wait, let me guess, you stayed out past curfew," a woman with overly bleached hair and wearing a tight, neon pink dress mocks me as she scoots closer to me on the metal bench I've been sitting on for the last several hours, waiting to get my one phone call.

"Nah, it was for killing a hooker." I scoot away from her because she smells like my house, and that's not a good thing.

She stares at me with her bloodshot eyes, confused at first, but then she laughs. "You're funny."

"I'm not trying to be funny," I mumble, putting more distance between us.

Her eyes narrow at me as her lips part. "You really don't want to start something with me, little girl. I got people out there that can make ya disappear."

"They'll have to get in line." With that, I drag my ass off the bench and wander over toward the bars at the front of the cell.

An instant later, a younger officer with short brown hair approaches the area. "Maddison Averly?"

I perk up at that. "Yeah, that's me."

He reaches for the keys that are clipped to the waistband of his belt. "You get one phone call."

"It's about damn time," I grumble, eliciting a scowl from him. "Sorry." I offer him a smile, to which seems to relax him a smidgeon.

"I'm Officer James," he tells me as he opens the door, the hinges creaking. "I'm going to take you to the phone so you can go call your mom or dad or whoever. While talking to them, make sure to have them come bail you out. It should only take a couple of hours to get everything done."

"Thanks." I pretend it'll be that easy, when it won't. At all. Not only because my mother will likely be drunk, so she'll have to sober up first, but she's probably broke. I have some money, but that means letting her know where I keep my stash of cash, and that could lead to a whole other set of problems.

After the officer shuts the door, he steers me past other barred cells, heading toward the front of the prison.

As I'm going over what I should say to my mother in my head, something in one of the cells captures my attention. Or, well, not something, but two guys to be exact.

They look close to my age and are absolutely gorgeous, but that's not what has me staring at them. No, it's the fact that every single detail about them screams that they're royals, which is what everyone in the city calls people from the southside.

I've lived on the poor side of the city for so many years that I rarely catch a glimpse of any royals. It's not even that that has me gawking at them. It's seeing two guys dressed in designer clothes, sitting next to men who are covered in grime and dirt, and one even has blood all over his shirt.

The two of them are night and day; one with hair paler than sunlight and the other has hair like the midnight sky. Where one is dressed in a button-down shirt, dress pants, and stylish sneakers, the other is sporting a black shirt, dark jeans, boots to die for, and a leather jacket that probably costs more than my mother's, father's, and everyone else's cars whom I know. They're also both wearing watches that sparkle even against the shitty lighting of the cell, and while the blond guy is smiling, the other has a grimace set so deeply into his expression I doubt it ever leaves his face.

However, despite their difference, their facial features bear resemblance, particularly the full lips and thick, dark eyelashes, so they are probably related. Not that I care. I'm merely fascinated, like when looking at panda bears in a zoo. Well, if panda bears could make intense eye contact, which the one with the dark hair suddenly does while the blond one keeps yammering away at him.

"I still can't believe we're in jail." Blondie laughs while shaking his head. "This is so wild. I mean, no one at school will believe us when we tell them. It'll make a hell of a story."

The dark-haired guy looks bored as hell—or annoyed. It's hard to tell. "We don't need to tell anyone." He keeps staring at me with his smoky-gray eyes. "And the only reason we're in here is because, like usual, you couldn't keep it in your pants."

I feel like he's daring me to look away, which is why I don't.

"Wait right here, and when he's done, make your call. You'll have five minutes, and then it'll cut you off," Officer James suddenly says as he comes to a stop.

I blink my eyes away from the gray ones and realize we've reached the payphone that's against the concrete wall, across from the cell the rich guys are in. A middle-aged, bald man, who looks like an accountant, is currently using it.

"I'm sorry, Mom," he's saying, "but I can't call Nadine, because she told me if I did it again, she'd file for a divorce." He starts to cry as he turns his back to me. "I don't ever mean to do it. I just can't help it ... I'm so messed up. She was just so beautiful, and I ..." He starts crying even louder. "I don't know why I keep doing this."

Great, he's a cheater, and he's on something.

God, this is so awkward, but the officer appears content about leaving me standing here as he wanders over to another officer, who I think was here the last time I got arrested, and starts chatting about the upcoming football season.

I slant against the wall and pretend like I can't feel gray eyes staring at me, watching me for whatever reason.

"I know, but I ..." The middle-aged man starts sobbing with his head lowered. "Please, Mommy Bear."

I side-eye him and pull a face. *Mommy Bear?* What the hell is this guy's damage?

As he keeps babbling and crying, I sneak a glance in gray eyes' direction and, yep, sure enough, he's still looking at me. And his brother is still talking.

Dude's a total Chatty Kathy.

"Come on, River; you have got to quit sulking about this shit, or this year will suck." He slumps back against the wall and loosens the red tie around his neck. "I know you're still upset about everything that went down, but this emo shit-funk you've been in is starting to be a real downer." Something Blondie says triggers gray eyes—who Blondie called River—and his nostrils flare. He starts to look away from me when his brother asks, "And what the hell are you even looking at back there?" He twists around and glances over. His eyes are bright blue, and he has a small scar underneath his eye that seems oddly out of place with the flawless appearance of the rest of him. When he spots me, a smile touches his lips. "Aw, the staring makes sense now."

Great, I've drawn way more attention than I prefer.

I could look away, but that's not how I roll. No, if I look away, this guy will think I'm intimidated by him. So, I carry his gaze and cross my arms.

He smirks, and then the dickhead winks at me.

I roll my eyes then pull a face, which causes his forehead to crease and a shocked sort of laugh to escape his lips. Then he gets up, makes his way over to me, and wraps his fingers around the bars as he smiles at me.

He's tall, but I am, too, so that's saying a lot. If I had to guess, I'd assume he was almost six inches taller than me, putting him at around six-foot-four.

"You know, I think that might be the first time anyone has returned my charming smile with a dirty look," Blondie says, appearing more pleased by this than he should.

"Well, since you're so clueless about the look, I'll let you in on the interpretation. It wasn't an open invitation for you to talk to me," I reply, propping my boot up against the wall. "It was the opposite."

He drags his teeth along his bottom lip. "I'm betting that mouth of yours got you in here."

"Better my mouth than what's between my legs," I say sweetly, recalling how River said something about them being in here because Blondie couldn't keep it in his pants.

His brows rise toward his hairline, his lips parting in shock. Then he hastily composes himself and opens his mouth to say who the hell knows what—I never find out because River speaks first.

"Finn, sit your ass back down," he demands from the bench

as he slants back and stares up at the ceiling. He isn't even looking in our direction, but irritation is flowing off of him. "Before you end up getting us into more trouble."

Finn arches a brow at me, that haughty grin still present. "I think that's my brother's way of saying you look like trouble."

"Your brother's smart," I inform him. "Because I am a huge pain in the ass and a load of trouble."

He eyes me over, and the smirk broadens. "Maybe, but you look like the fun kind of trouble."

"I'm not," I assure him. I'm also well aware that this guy is flirting with me. I've been hit on more than my fair share of times, but having a royal flirt with me is definitely new. "I'm the more boring kind of trouble." I trace my finger across my chest in an X pattern. "Cross my heart."

He chuckles, his eyes crinkling around the corners.

I internally sigh. I'm trying to get him to be annoyed with me, yet I'm somehow doing the exact opposite.

"Why did you get put in here, for reals?" he wonders, his eyes sparkling with curiosity.

"For castrating a royal." I smirk when he visibly winces.

"I think you're lying."

"Then why did you wince?"

"Because you said the word castration," he replies in all seriousness. "All guys have a physical reaction to that word. Even castrated ones."

I almost laugh and, holy shit, I don't like that at all. I do not need to be laughing at some rich guy, even if he's funny, and gorgeous, and charming. But that's the thing. The charm is fake.

I've heard stories about royal men slipping into the shadows of the northside and wining and dining women from there, only to ditch them once they've used them up. I've even heard stories about them knocking women up then disowning the baby. My aunt Ellie told me that happened to her friend and said it destroyed her. She had to give the baby up for adoption and everything because she couldn't afford to take care of her and had no support system.

I try to come up with some snotty response that hopefully gets him to leave me alone, but come up empty.

Fortunately, the middle-aged man hangs up the phone. He faces me with tears streaming down his face and snot running out of his nose. "I think my marriage is over."

"It's a good thing you'll have your Mommy Bear." I push away from the wall.

I don't feel bad for being rude. My dad has cheated on my mom more times than I can count, and it's turned her into a shell of a human being. I used to wish she'd leave him—and I still do—but I'm trying to disconnect with the situation because I've spent way too many years and energy trying to convince her to, and it's gotten me nowhere.

Tears bubble in his eyes that are bloodshot and shadowed, and he reeks of booze and smoke. Everything about him screams strung out, and I hate the familiarity of his presence.

"You're a bitch. You know that?" he spits, stepping toward me.

I keep my feet planted on the floor. "So I've been told."

He balls his hands into fists—to hit me, perhaps—but I never get to find out since Officer James returns.

"Gary," he says to the middle-aged man, "your time's up. Let's get you put back in the cell."

"But I don't wanna go in there," he whines while tugging at the bottom of his shirt, like a toddler about to have a tantrum. "It smells bad."

"You smell just like it," Officer James assures him, causing me to snort a laugh.

When Officer James glances at me, I offer him an apologetic look, like I did before. It wins him over again, and he tries not to smile before urging the middle-aged guy—aka Gary—toward the barred door to the cell the royals are in.

Lucky them.

Tearing my attention off the cell, I pick up the phone and, with a deep breath, dial my mom's cell.

"Please pick up. Please pick up," I mumble, crossing my fingers.

If she doesn't, I'm so screwed since it's Friday night and all my friends will more than likely be too wasted to come down. My aunt Ellie lives outside the country and is unreachable, and I don't know my other relatives. And Kelsie, who I consider my best friend, took off a handful of weeks ago with this guy who has a warrant out for his arrest. She says he's the love of her life, but she's flakey when it comes to guys. I know she'll be back eventually—

"Hey ... who is this?" my mom answers the phone, and I immediately sense she's been drinking.

"This is Maddy, Mom." I pause. "Are you drunk?" I lower my head against the wall. The concrete is cold against my skin and is likely covered in all sorts of gross substances, but it fits the moment.

"Nah, I've just had a few beers. That's all," she insists.

"Well, you sound drunk," I mumble, noting the music playing in the background. "Where are you?"

"I'm at the bar," she replies. "But I've only been here for like an hour. I promise I'm not that drunk."

"Okay." I'm not sure if I believe her, but I need to get bailed out, and she doesn't sound completely drunk, so she's probably my best bet. "I need a favor from you, and it needs to be done quickly."

"What's wrong?" she instantly asks. "You didn't run into that gang, did you? The one that's upset with your father because they think he got their boss in trouble."

The way she says "they think" makes my lips twitch. She's always so delusional when it comes to my father, but now's not the time to get into this with her.

"I did, actually," I tell her. "They didn't hurt me or anything, but I got arrested."

"Shit, did you hit someone again?"

"Only because they were holding me against my will."

"Dammit, Mads, why do you have to keep doing this?" She has the audacity to scold me. "I thought you learned the first time that you can't get into fights. You have to be more careful."

Breathe in. Breathe out.

Go to your state of Zen.

Think of running. And fresh air. And open space.

"Can you come bail me out?" I ask.

She hesitates. "I don't have the money, hon. You might have to wait this out."

"I can't wait it out, Mom. I have work tomorrow and school stuff to deal with."

"Well, I don't know what to tell you. Money doesn't grow on trees."

She says this all the time, even though she's never given me a dime. Even when I was a child, she'd often send me to the corner of the street to beg for money. When things got really bad, I'd turn to stealing, something I'm not proud of. The moment I turned fifteen, though, and was of legal age to become employed, I got a job, and it was a relief.

"I know that, but you're always able to come up with money to bail Dad out," I remind her. "Can't you just use your car title to get a bail bond?"

"Oh, I took a loan out on that a few weeks ago, so I can't."

I feel like banging my head against the wall. "For what?"

"Just for stuff," she replies as someone says something to her. She laughs, and it's like nails on a chalkboard. "Look, I'm really sorry you're in jail, but I can't bail you out, so ..."

I shut my eyes and breathe in and out. "Look, I have some money stashed away, and I'll tell you where it is, but you have to swear that you'll only take the amount to bail me out because the rest of it is for my school expenses. If you take any extra, I swear I'll disown you and never talk to you or help you again."

"Jesus, Mads, what kind of mother do you think I am?" She

sounds appalled, as if she's conveniently forgotten the multiple times she's screwed me over.

"I'm serious, Mom," I warn. "Don't take anything extra than five hundred, which should be enough to bail me out."

I'm unsure of what I'll do after I get out, seeing as how I might face assault charges. Maybe I can talk to Drew and see if I can get him to drop the charges. It's a long shot, but I do have some dirt on him that could help me, like how he steals some of the money from dealing. And if his boss finds out ... well, Drew could end up in the canal with the trash. I wouldn't tell his boss —I don't want blood on my hands—but I could threaten to do so.

"I promise I won't," my mother reassures me, and I loathe the doubt plaguing my mind.

"The money is taped to the upper part of my top drawer," I tell her, hoping I'm not making a mistake. I used to keep my cash in a checking account, but then my debit card got stolen while I was at school—twice—so I decided to hide my money and only carry a low amount on me. That way, if I ever get robbed, I won't lose that much money. "It's in a leather pouch. Take five hundred, and then put the rest back, okay?"

"Okay," she tells me as the sounds in the background switches.

"And leave right now to do it," I add.

"I'm taking off right now, hon. See you in a bit." She hangs up.

And I'm left with this twisting sensation in my stomach that I've felt way too many times, but I do my best to disregard it, hang up the phone, and turn around to tell Officer James I'm ready to go back to the cell.

Finn has retaken his seat, but his attention is still on me, and a hint of pity is in his eyes, meaning he probably overheard that sad conversation that is my life. Whatever. Like I give a shit that some rich dude I'll never see again heard me arguing with my mother about not robbing me.

River, however, has his head resting against the cement wall, and his eyes are shut. Is he seriously asleep right now? I mean ... how? It smells, and it's loud, and I think a guy inside his cell is peeing in the corner.

"You good?" Officer James appears in my line of vision.

I nod and force a smile onto my face. "Yeah, my mom's heading down to get me."

"Good." He nods for me to follow him as he heads back toward the cell I was in. "Do you mind if I ask how old you are?"

I warily eye him over as I follow him. "Eighteen ... Why?"

He holds up his hand. "I promise I'm not being a pervert. It's just that you look like you're around the age you should be going to college, but you're in here, and I'm wondering why."

"You act like there aren't a lot of eighteen-year-olds that come in here," I point out. "This is northside—over half the people my age have probably been in here, if not more."

"I know, but you don't have that same roughness to you that a lot of others have." He stops in front of the cell door. "My partner back there says you've been arrested before, but that he doesn't think you're a bad kid. That you've just been dealt a bad hand."

"Mmm ... A bad hand? Is that what this nightmare of a life is?"

He sympathetically looks at me as he reaches for his keys. "Look, I've been there. I grew up in northside, too, but just because you were born into a shitty life, doesn't mean you need to keep living it." He pulls the door open.

This might be the first time I've ever liked a police officer.

"Thanks for the advice, Officer James." I step into the cell. "Just so you know, I'm trying to not live this shitty life anymore. I'm going to college in just a few days, then I'm out of this city."

His lips tug into a smile. "Good for you, kid. I hope everything works out for you."

Me, too, James; me, too.

Right now, though, I'm just hoping my mother doesn't screw me over.

THREE
MADDISON

My mom screwed me over.

It took about two hours of me sitting in the cell to realize this, but I tried to deny it for another hour. At the stroke of midnight, however, my carriage of denial melted into infuriating reality.

This is only confirmed when Officer James walks by my cell, and I ask him if my mother has shown up at all. He tells me he'll check, and when he returns, the look on his face says it all.

"She hasn't yet." He stands in front of the cell with pity in his eyes, which is the second time I've seen that look tonight. "Maybe she went to the wrong station. It happens sometimes."

"She knows where to go. She's more familiar with this building than the bar." Shaking my head, I return to the bench. "She screwed me over. Again." I let my head fall back against the wall hard enough that it hurts.

"Do you need to call someone else?" Officer James wonders. "You can get another phone call if you request it."

I shake my head from side to side. "There's no one else to call."

"I ..." He trails off as another officer approaches him.

They talk for a second, and then the officer hurries off.

Officer James gives me a remorseful look. "I have to take care of some stuff, but I'll swing by in a bit and check on you." He pats the bars. "Try to think of someone else to call, okay? You don't want to be in here for days."

I give him a thumbs-up, and he jogs off, keys jingling on his belt.

"You could always suck his dick," the woman with bleached hair says. "He might let you out if you did."

We're the only two people left in the cell, and it's been quiet, for the most part. I've been grateful for that.

"Leave me alone, Nadine," I mutter with my eyes shut. "I'm not going to suck anyone's dick. And besides, he seems like a nice guy."

She snorts a laugh. "Yeah, because you're at the ripe young age of just legal. If you were ten years older, he wouldn't even acknowledge your existence."

Sighing, I crack an eye open and look at her. "I get that a lot of guys are assholes, but I don't think he is."

She releases a condescending laugh. "You naïve little girl. All men are assholes. And the sooner you realize that, the better your life will be, because you can use it to your benefit." With that, she stands up, and her heels click against the floor as she wanders to the bars. "Hey, Officer Tony, come get me out of here, and I'll suck your dick for free," she calls out.

An instant later, a fifty-year-old man with gray hair and a beard approaches the cell. "What was that, Nadine?" he questions with a firm tone, but the corners of his lips threaten to turn upward.

She reaches through the bars and rubs him. "You heard what I said."

I expect him to push her away, but he reaches for his keys instead. "I was waiting for you to get tired of being in here." He unlocks the door and opens it.

Nadine winks at me before sauntering out.

As I sit there with my jaw hanging to my knees, Officer Tony fixes his gaze on me as he's locking the cell back up. "You new here?" He twists the key in the lock.

"Nope," is all I say.

I can tell what he wants, and I'm *so* not going there.

He narrows his eyes. "If you know what's good for you, you'll keep your mouth shut about this."

My lips remain fused, and he blasts me with a nasty look before hurrying off with his hand on the small of Nadine's back.

"Yuck," I mutter with an exaggerated shudder. Then I slump back against the wall and start waiting out my time.

For the next ten minutes or so, I sit in peaceful silence, lamely attempting to convince myself that maybe my mom just forgot to bail out. Or perhaps something happened to her. Deep down, the truth brutally sits in my stomach like a bad case of diarrhea.

I'm tired, hungry, and one step away from lying down on the dirty bench so I can attempt to sleep off this shitty night when footsteps approach my cell again. I expect it to be Nadine and Officer Tony, but it's Officer James again, and he's wearing a bright smile. It makes me a bit uneasy as I recall what Nadine said right before she left.

"I have good news, kid," he informs me, and it's kind of funny he calls me "kid" when he's not that much older than me. "You made bail."

So much relief washes over me as I stand up and hurry over to the door. "My mom showed up?" My shock is evident in my tone.

He sticks the key into the lock. "No, an anonymous person paid for it." He pulls open the door.

Confusion webs through me. "What? What does that even mean?"

He clasps the keys back to his belt. "It means the person who paid your bail doesn't want you to know who it is."

Seriously, what the heck is going on here?

"But you know who it is?"

He hesitantly nods. "I do. But legally, I can't tell you."

I stand in the doorway, stunned, with my jaw basically bitch-smacking the concrete. Who the hell would pay for my bail? I don't even know anyone who could afford to.

"Don't overthink it," he tells me with a smile. "Just make the most of it, okay?"

I assess him. "Did you pay my bail?"

He chuckles, his eyes crinkling around the corners. "Nah, I

don't have that kind of money. But I do know that when life hands you a good thing, you should be thankful and pay it forward, even if it is by doing something good with your own life."

I assess him again then grin. "You really are a regular after-school special, aren't you, Officer James?"

He laughs as we make our way toward the exit.

As we pass by the men's holding cell, I note the royals are gone. I'm not surprised. They were probably bailed out hours ago because they can afford it.

"Nah, I just like to try to remain positive. Life's too short to let the dark shit eat you up, you know?" Officer James types in a passcode on the security box beside the thick exit door that leads to my sweet, blissful freedom. "I do hope I don't see you again. No offense intended."

"None taken," I reply as the door beeps open. The chatter from the other side is like sweet music to my ears. "Because I feel the same way." Then I step through the door, feeling lighter, which is weird considering I'm walking out of jail. But I've never had something like this happen to me, where I'm handed a freebie with no strings attached. And, while most of me is dubious that a catch is hidden in this gift, a tiny part of me wonders if I'm finally getting a break.

THAT POSITIVE OUTLOOK on life goes straight into the canal when I return home. My mom is MIA, and the house is quiet and a mess, like someone ransacked through everything. What they were looking for is beyond me since we own nothing but a holey sofa, a cracked kitchen table, and a few lamps. The only valuable item is my money, and it's gone—all of it. My mom cleaned me out. She even stole all my change.

"Dammit." I kick my wood-panel bedroom wall then slump to the floor. Between work and getting ready for school, cleaning up hasn't been a priority, so clothes, makeup, shoes, and some food wrappers are scattered across the carpet.

I need to shower and clean the place up, but my mood and energy level are at zero. And not only over the money. I haven't slept in over twenty-four hours, so sleep deprivation is kicking in. I need to get some rest, but it's not an option. Neither is cleaning. What I need is take a quick shower and come up with a starting point to begin my search for my mother dearest. Because, while there is a chance she may have spent all of my cash by now, if she hasn't, I need to get it back. If I don't, I can kiss going to college goodbye.

I grab a pair of clean, cut-off shorts, a tank top, a pair of underwear, and a bra before hurrying into the bathroom and turning on the shower.

The small space is also a mess, with toiletries and towels thrown everywhere, and a handful of pills have been dumped across the yellow-stained linoleum floor. The place looks like when my father would run out of drugs and desperately begin to rip the house apart in his strung-out state, convinced that he somehow accidentally forgot where he hid his stash. While I was the one who had to clean up afterward, I'd let him go on for as long as he wanted to since, once he gave up, he'd invest all of that restless energy into screaming and hitting me.

"Where'd you hide them?" he once screamed in my face. "I know you took them, Maddison! They don't just disappear."

I was eight years old and cowering in the corner of the living room by the floor lamp that he had just broken, hugging my knees to my chest, as if balling myself up would protect me. It didn't. Nothing ever did. And a moment later, he smacked me across the face so hard my ears rang.

My chest ached, and my eyes burned, but I didn't cry. In fact, I didn't make a sound, not wanting to escalate the situation further.

He let out a scream with his hands balled to the side. "I hate this place, and I hate this family so much!" Then he reeled around and stormed out of the house, slamming the door behind him with so much force a glass on the table fell onto the floor and shattered into pieces.

"What the hell did you do?" my mother asked, rushing into the living room. Her eyes were swollen, she had a welt on her cheek, and she curled her hands into fists as she assessed me and the broken glass. "Why do you have to bother him when he's upset?" she shrieked, her face bright red, her eyes bloodshot. "Goddammit, Maddison, I told you to stay away from him."

"He found me," I pointed out, my tone hollow and familiar.

"Well, you should've hidden better." She shook her head then looked at me with disgust. "Clean up the glass." With that, she spun around and stormed into her room, slamming the door behind her.

Then I was alone. And while it was lonely, peace wrapped around me, like my lungs could thrive again.

Tearing myself from the memory, I climb into the shower and scrub my body down then wash my face and hair. I break record time and am hopping out less than five minutes later.

I hurriedly get dressed, not bothering to dry my hair or put makeup on. Then I collect my house keys and wallet with the plan to go to the bar that I believe my mother was at when I called her. If she's not there, I'll ask around and see if anyone saw her or heard her say anything that would offer me a clue as to where she went. As I slip my shoes on, though, someone knocks on the door.

Strange. People rarely stop by since my dad has been in jail.

I slowly get up from the sofa and go to the living room window, where the dusty curtain is drawn shut. Carefully, I pull it back and peek outside.

Standing near the front door of my apartment is a taller guy wearing a hoodie with the hood drawn over his head. While shadows mostly conceal his face, it's clear the monstrosity of a figure has to be Drew.

I curse under my breath as my gaze sweeps the front area of the apartment complex. As I suspected, more people are hanging around in the parking lot beside an old, beat-up red car —two more guys and a girl to be exact. All of them are wearing hoodies, and they're causally glancing in this direction.

They have to be the same people who tried to jump me earlier.

This is so bad.

I move away from the window and duck down, even though there's no way they can see me with the curtain closed. But the anxiety of them being just outside has me wanting to hide.

I crawl back to my room and quietly shut the door as Drew knocks again, this time with more force.

"Mads!" he calls out. "Just come out, and let's get this over with, okay?"

"Yeah, Scar Man, I'll get right on that," I mumble under my breath as I sink onto my bed.

Another loud knock.

And another.

And my hope that I'll be able to stop my mother from spending all of my money dwindles with each one.

Eventually, my eyelids grow too heavy to stay awake anymore, and I surrender into the darkness of sleep, a tiny part of me wishing I never had to wake up again, because I'd take the hellish nightmares over the hell of the reality that is my life.

FOUR
RIVER

Do you ever get the feeling that your life is one big joke? Only the punchline is never delivered, so you never get to laugh about it?

That's how I feel all the damn time, like I'm living in a joke, just waiting for the laugh, but it never arrives.

"Stop stressing," my twin brother Finn says as we're let out of the jail cell. "Dad won't find out about this."

"Doubtful," I mutter as we follow the officer toward the exit door. "A hundred bucks says when we exit this building, paparazzi will be outside."

He wavers before saying, "Maybe there's a back exit." He looks at the officer as he's opening the door. "Hey man, is there another way out of this place? Like maybe a more lowkey way out?"

The officer gives him an annoyed look. "No." He yanks

open the door, muttering, "Damn rich brats thinking they can always get what they want."

I internally sigh as I follow Finn through the doorway and into the check-out area. This isn't our first time in jail, but we've never been arrested for anything I've done. I'm the good one, my father is always telling me. The obedient one.

And perhaps I am, but only because my future is headed to a pointless abyss. Finn constantly tells me that I'm depressed, and he might be right. But I don't know how to fix myself when I've got nothing to look forward to.

"What an asshole," Finn says as he collects his wallet from off the counter.

"Careful," I warn. "They can still throw you back in jail."

He makes a big show of rolling his eyes as he stuffs his wallet into the back pocket of his pants.

I sigh again. It's kind of my thing when I'm around my brother.

As I collect my belongings from the counter, Finn wanders to the waiting room area that's buzzing with chatter. For some reason, my mind drifts to that girl we saw while we were behind bars. She looked so upset when she was making the phone call, like her whole world was breaking apart, but she was fighting to keep it together.

It almost felt like looking in a mirror. Although, I'm sure our problems are much different.

Still, I can't stop thinking about her, her big eyes so full of sadness, her long, flowing hair, and the tough demeanor she was throwing at Finn.

Then I think about how worried she looked when the phone call ended. Clearly, she was concerned her mother wouldn't come bail her out.

"Hey... um... I have a question," I say to the middle-aged woman with blonde hair sitting behind the desk.

The phone is ringing in the background and she looks irritated as she looks at me. "What is it?"

I rest my arms on the counter and offer her a friendly smile, which softens her a bit. It's something I've learned how to do over the years—charm people with my smiles and good looks. Finn is way better at it, though, and does it more frequently. But he can also act on his flirting. I can't.

"There's this girl back in one of those cells," I say. "She's probably around my age. She has dark hair, is tall, and really pretty."

"Okay," she replies. "What's the question?"

I shift my weight. "I was just wondering if she made bail, and if not, I'd like to pay for hers."

Her brows rise in surprise, but quickly even out. "Let me see if I can figure out who it is." She rotates her chair toward the computer and clicks a few keys. "There's only one young woman in the holding cell right now. The other two are much older."

"That's got to be her then." I reach to retrieve my wallet out of my back pocket. "How much is her bail?"

"It'll be about five hundred dollars." She watches my reaction.

I don't even blink as I take out my card. Money has never

been a struggle for me. It's the strings connected to it that have caused the issues.

She smiles as she grabs the card, but I detect the slightest bit of detesting envy in her eyes. This happens a lot, especially on northside.

"And can you keep this anonymous?" I ask, not wanting anyone to find out about this.

She nods and then swipes my card.

A few minutes later, I'm approaching Finn in the waiting room.

"What's that look on your face for?" he questions, zipping up his jacket.

"What look?" I question, glancing at my watch.

It's late and I'm hoping that'll lower the risk of paparazzi loitering outside.

Finn lifts a brow at me. "Okay, play dumb then. But just an FYI, you're not very good at it." He throws me a grin as he backs toward the glass exit doors that lead outside. "I am, but you're not bro."

He's right. Finn is great at fitting in wherever he is. Me? I stand out like a single cloud in a sunny sky. I've been deemed the brooding one, the intense one—the untouchable one.

"I'm not playing dumb," I try to lie to him anyway as we push out the doors and step into the crisp night air—

Flash.

Click.

Flash.

Blinding lights flicker across the darkness blanketing the outside.

"River, over here," a guy holding a camera says.

I look the opposite way and find more cameras pointed at me.

The paparazzi have found out, which means our father will find out about our little outing tonight.

We've been caught and the consequences are going to be brutal.

FIVE
MADDISON

Music is booming through the house, the volume so deafening that the floors vibrate with the bass thumping. Usually, I like music, but the sound of laughter and the occasional shrieking, manic laughter has me on edge.

My parents are having a party, like they do every weekend. During these times, I'm instructed to lock myself in my room. Normally, I'm okay with that, but this particular party sounds like a bunch of lunatics have locked themselves in a padded room and are going insane. They've also been at it for over twelve hours, and I'm hungry, bored, and I have to pee.

Finally, I can't take it anymore. Standing up from my bed, I pad over to my bedroom door and unlock it. Then, sucking in a breath, I open the door. I immediately get overwhelmed by the stench of smoke and rotting food. But that's pretty typical for my house, so I ignore it and step out into the hallway. A couple is making out just a ways down, but they're too distracted to notice me, so I make a beeline into the bathroom and lock the door behind me.

I use the bathroom as quickly as I can, wash my hands, and then prepare to run back into my room. I wish I could grab something to eat from the kitchen, but if my parents see me doing so, they will be so mad. Plus, there's a huge chance we're out of food, anyway.

I can't wait until school on Monday. At least there I can get something to eat—

Knock. Knock. Knock.

I tense as someone knocks on the bathroom door.

I'm unsure if I should say anything since I'm supposed to be in my room.

Knock. Knock. Knock.

"Maddy," a man says through the door.

I remain frozen. Who the heck is out there?

"Maddy girl, it's me, your dad's friend, Brock," the man says through the door. "Open up. I'm supposed to take you to get something to eat."

I hesitate. I know Brock. He hangs around here a lot, and he seems nice. Plus, my dad and him are close. It's weird, though, that he'd take me to get something to eat when no one ever does.

Knock. Knock. Knock.

"Knock, knock, knock, Maddy," he says as he knocks. "Come on, sweetie; open the door. I know you've gotta be starving by now."

Biting my lip, I reach for the doorknob ...

Knock. Knock. Knock—

Knock. Knock. Knock.

My eyelids spring open. For a heart-soaring instant, I still think I'm seven years old and back in that bathroom. But sluggishly, the haziness of sleep evaporates from my body, and I realize I'm eighteen years old, lying in my bed, and someone is banging on the door.

Could it still be Drew? How much time has gone by since I fell asleep?

Sitting up, I reach for my phone and check the time. "Holy crap, I slept for like twelve hours." I can't even remember the last time that happened.

Knock. Knock. Knock.

I consider letting the knocking continue until Drew gets bored and leaves, but what if it isn't Drew? I should probably check.

I exit my bedroom, pad to the living room window, and I'm pulling back the curtain right as the person knocks again. I blink several times against the bright sunlight shining down from the cloudless sky before seeing anything. And once I can, I'm so damn perplexed because standing in front of my apartment door is a man and woman who I've never seen before. What makes the entire situation so bizarre is that they're dressed in formal attire; the man wearing a pressed suit and tie, and the woman a pencil shirt and button-down silk blouse. They look straight out of a business magazine and out of place in this dump of an apartment complex. Maybe they have the wrong place?

Letting go of the curtain, I walk over to the front door and open it as the woman is about to knock again.

She startles mid-knock then lowers her hand and smiles at me. "Are you Maddison Averly?"

"Um ... yeah?" In the pit of my mind, concern is rising that they're here because my mother did something terrible or illegal.

"Oh, good." A smile remains painted on her lips. "Your last address listed in the system hasn't been updated in years, so we weren't positive if you still lived here." Her phone rings, and she fetches it out, her gaze scrolling over the screen.

"I've lived here for most of my life," I inform her, glancing at the man from the corner of my eye. He's staring at me with arms crossed, and while he has sunglasses on, I can tell he's assessing me.

This is too damn strange.

I direct my attention back at the woman as she puts her phone back into her jacket pocket. "Who are you?" I ask. "And why are you looking for me?"

"Because we have some great news for you, Maddison." Her smile is starting to creep me out. "Have you ever heard of the Royal Academy?"

I lean against the doorjamb, on guard and totally confused. "Of course I have. I may be on the trashy side of town, but I do read news articles on occasion." Anyone who does knows about Royal Academy, a highly elite college located on the outskirts of the southside of the city where only wealthy people of royal bloodlines can attend. Royal City has a lot of royal families that reside in the area, hence the name.

"Oh yes, of course you do. I wasn't implying that you didn't know how to read." She grows flustered. "In fact, we're well aware of how intelligent you are—a straight-A student and all-star track athlete."

"I'm not that smart," I stress. "It's easy to get straight A's in northside schools." And that's the sad truth. Lower class means a lower education due to lack of funding.

Yep, Social Darwinism at its finest.

"Don't underestimate yourself." She tries to sound encouraging. "We're viewed your test scores. You're an exceptional student and athlete, and you're going to make a great addition to the academy."

It takes my brain a moment to process what she said. "Wait ... What?"

"You've been selected by our client to receive a scholarship for the Royal Academy," the man finally speaks. "It will cover room and board, and all of your tuition and book fees for the next four years."

My gaze shifts between the two of them, and then I laugh. "Okay, who put you up to this?" Before either of them responds, a thought slams into my mind that makes me stiffen. "Wait—did Drew and his gang have you do this to lure me out of the house?"

It seems like too much of a creative plan for Drew and his gang, but it could be possible. The woman does sort of look familiar. Then again, her face is relatively generic. I move to shut the door, anyway.

"Wait," the woman calls out. "We're not here to lure you out of the house. I don't know who Drew or his gang is, and I assure you this is real."

"Bullshit," I call her out. "The Royal Academy doesn't just hand out scholarships. Like I said, I read the news; I know the deal. Only the rich and royal go there. There are no lower-class pity handouts. And even if in some weird alternate realm there was, I'm not the sort of person who'd be lucky enough to get one."

She inches closer to the door. "This isn't luck. Our client decided last year that he wanted to handpick one student from the northside and give them the opportunity of a lifetime. He spent months sorting through school records, trying to find the perfect candidate, and he selected you based on your achievements."

My skepticism stays present. "Did those records also tell you I'm on probation and am currently facing assault charges? Because that doesn't seem like much of an achievement."

"He's well aware of your probation status, and he was informed this morning about the charges that were filed against you last night," she tells me then looks at the man. "Give her the envelope, Bruce. She clearly needs proof." She snaps her fingers at him.

Bruce barely shifts his stance as he sticks his hand into his suit jacket, retrieves a blue envelope, and hands it to me.

Written across the front, in perfect cursive handwriting, is

"*Maddison Averly,*" and the back is sealed with the wax seal of a crown stamp—the Royal Academy's logo.

"There's more paperwork you'll have to fill out," the woman explains, "but this is an official invitation. Once you've accepted it, we'll take you down to the office where we can cross the T's and dot the I's, and make everything official."

The envelope looks legitimate, but wariness nibbles at my insides.

"Who's your client?" I smooth my thumb over the wax seal.

"He'd like to remain anonymous," she clarifies. "This is something he's chosen to do out of pure kindness and nothing more. If word gets out who he is, it'll become a publicity stunt."

Anonymous, just like the person who bailed me out of jail. Could this be the same person?

Although, she said her client found out about my new arrest charges this morning ...

I don't know ... This entire thing is weird as hell. It can't be real? How could it be? My life sucks. It's supposed to suck. I've accepted that it probably will for quite a while. So, how can something like this be happening to me?

I need a minute or two to process this and also to see if it could even be legit.

"Can I have some time to think this over?" I ask without opening the envelope.

Surprise flickers in her eyes. "Um ... Sure." She tucks a strand of red hair behind her ear. "But I can only give you a day at most since classes start next Wednesday."

"Okay, I'll let you know no later than tomorrow if I will

accept it." And I'll spend the rest of the day figuring out if this is real because it can't be.

It just can't.

I search for signs of Drew and his gang lurking in the parking lot, convinced they're behind this. Not a sign of them is in sight, though. However, a sleek, black Mercedes is parked amid the rusted cars and beat-up trucks.

The woman takes a card from her pocket and gives it to me. "This is my contact information. My name is Bethany, and this is my colleague, Bruce. We work for the Royal Fairland Law Firm down on Main. Call me when you're ready to accept, and you can come down to the office and sign the paperwork." She says it with such certainty, like there's no way I won't accept.

And why wouldn't I? It's a great opportunity.

And yet, I can't get past this inkling it's a big prank.

"Sounds good." I force a smile onto my face.

She returns it then says goodbye before endeavoring toward the parking lot with Bruce trailing behind her. Not surprising, they climb into the Mercedes, which also removes the probability that Drew and his friends are behind this, unless they stole the vehicle, but that's a little extreme, even for them.

Stepping back, I shut and lock the door. Then I return to my room, sink onto the unmade bed, lean against the headboard, and turn the envelope over, staring at the wax seal. I don't tear the envelope open, my distrust for this situation flowing potently through me.

It makes no sense that I'd be selected for this type of thing.

Not to mention I've never heard of someone from northside getting chosen for a scholarship

I set the envelope down without opening it and open my internet browser on my phone while examining Bethany's business card. Then I type in the name of the company she works for.

Tons of articles pop up, along with the business website. It's a highly prestigious law firm with a high-profile clientele. The more I scroll through the information online, the more skeptical I become that Drew and his gang are behind this. Creating business cards, hiring a woman and man to show up at my house, stealing a Mercedes, buying a wax stamp of the Royal Academy Crest—I highly doubt the guy voted the biggest procrastinator in high school is behind this project.

Diving deeper into my investigation, I search the Royal Academy. The website is the first thing to pop up, so I click on it. I've seen glimpses of it from some regions of northside and in photos that are attached to articles, but I forgot how castle-esque it is, with towers that peak to the sky, glistening, golden-trimmed columns, and a wide staircase that leads to the arched entrance. And that's just the outside view. The inside is equally as beautiful, with marble floors, cathedral ceilings, spiral stairways, and crystal chandeliers. Not to mention the highly sought-after professors, and the list of classes is beyond anything I could come up with in my wildest imagination.

Suddenly, it crashes into me like a car wreck. I could go to this place and get the education I never dreamed of, only to avoid disappointment. It's how I've lived my life—with low expectations because anything else would crush me.

But what if this is all real? What if I could go here?

I toss my phone aside, draw my knees to my chest, and yank my fingers through my hair, absolutely terrified.

It's ridiculous, I know, to be terrified of getting something great. But that's the thing about living on northside—you get so used to everything being awful that anything good almost feels like a threat.

SIX

MADDISON

It's been an hour, and the envelope Bethany gave me is currently sitting on my bed, unopened. I've been distracting myself by calling up friends of my mother's and a few bar owners to see if they've seen her. Every answer is the same.

"Sorry, Mads, but I haven't seen her," the owner of a bar my mother frequently hangs out at tells me. "Have you tried Larry's bar? She's been going there lately."

I pace the living room. "Yeah, I tried there already, and no one's seen her."

"I'm sure she'll show up eventually," he assures me. "She always does."

He's right, but she also stole almost two thousand dollars from me, and that's more money than she's ever had in her life. She could be doing all sorts of crazy things. Hell, she could've left the city.

"But if I do see her," he says, "I'll have her call you."

"Thanks." I hang up and slump into the lumpy sofa, weighed down by defeat.

To distract myself, I call up the police department to see if I can persuade the receptionist to divulge who paid my bail because it's been driving me absolutely insane.

"I'm sorry, hon," she tells me. "I can't give out that information since the person who paid for it wants to remain anonymous."

I blow out a frustrated exhale. "Fine, but can you at least tell me when my court date is?"

Click. Click. Click. I hear her typing on the keyboard.

"Sorry, it's not in the system yet," she replies. "But you can try to call back in a few days. Our systems are slow here."

"Okay, thanks." I hang up and rake my fingers through my hair.

Why would anyone do this for me? Who would do this for me?

I think about the lady who showed up on my doorstep, wondering if the two could be connected. I could open the envelope, but I'm still hesitant. Instead, I check my emails, but that only leaves me in more of a downer mood due to the email I receive from Royal City Community College.

DEAR MADDISON AVERLY,

It has been brought to our attention that you're currently on probation and, unfortunately, we can no longer award you with the high achievement scholarship. We're a school that prides itself on bringing in outstanding students who excel both in school, in athletics, and their personal lives. You will still be able to attend as a regular student. However, you will have to pay the tuition fees by Aug. 15th or you will be dropped from the classes you're currently enrolled in ...

I DROP my phone as shock whips through me. They took my scholarship away? Are they kidding me? I can't afford to pay for class. And it's bullshit because I know people who have been on probation who have gotten scholarships there.

Everything I worked so hard for is crumbling into a pile of dirt right in front of me, like the layer of dust coating the shaggy orange carpet. Well, maybe it's not crumbling. Perhaps I'm being shoved in a different direction.

Getting up, I go to my room, pick up the envelope, and tear it open. Inside is a piece of paper trimmed with inky gold and shimmering glitter.

DEAR MADDISON AVERLY,

We are pleased to accept you into the Royal Academy, where our goal is to give you the best education possible. We're ranked as the best college in the entire country. Upon accepting this invitation, you will be given an advisor to guide you through the next four years until graduation.

. . .

I STARE at the letter for a while, wishing I had someone to talk to about this. When I was younger, I used to talk to my aunt Ellie about my problems. Before she moved out of the country, she'd stop by and visit at least once every two months. Her visits were something I looked forward to because she'd bring me food and sometimes even a present, like the necklace she gave me. It's a crown-shaped pendant with a black diamond embedded into it. It's old and scratched up, but I still love it.

"Where did you get this?" I'd asked because it was the prettiest thing I'd ever seen.

"I've had it for a while," she replied. "But I don't wear it anymore, so I thought you'd like it."

I was beyond excited as I fumbled to get it on. "Thank you, Aunt Ellie."

"One day, I'm going to get you out of here, Maddy," she said as she helped me clasp it.

"How?" I wondered, wishing she could do it but feeling hopeless that something that wonderful could ever happen.

"I'm not sure yet," she told me. "But I promise you I will."

I haven't heard from her in about a year, and the last time she checked in, the conversation was short. She sounded nervous, telling me that she might be canceling her phone service, and she'd let me know if she did. Being uneasy wasn't completely uncommon for her, and I often wondered—still do— if she did something illegal for work since she was always so vague about her employment.

I've tried to call her a few times, but the number has been disconnected. I attempted to get her new number from my mother, but it was clear she had no clue her sister had changed her number.

Still, feeling desperate, I dial the last number I know belonged to her.

"I'm sorry, but this number has been disconnected," the recording tells me with a *beep*.

Gritting my teeth, I hang up the phone. If I could get a hold of my aunt, I know what she'd say.

"Take it, Mads," she'd tell me. "Because opportunities like this are a rarity in this world."

Before I can chicken out, I pick up the law firm card and dial Bethany's number.

"Hello, Bethany Mapleton, how may I help you?" she answers.

I summon a deep breath, knowing what I'm about to do will change the course of my life forever. "Hi, this is Maddison, and I'd like to accept the offer."

It should feel fantastic, and yet, even after all my research, doubt plagues my mind that this is too good to be true.

But I have no other choice except to hope it's just that.

Never in a million years did I think I'd be sitting in a cab, driving up the paved road that leads to the castle-esque building I've seen from a distance but never up close. And up close, it's breathtaking, with towers, ivory columns, and a gated entrance. Just behind that is an expansive stairway that stretches up to the entrance of the school, and peaking up toward the sky is the widest set of doors I've ever seen.

And don't even get me started on the landscape, with grass and trees so flourishing they look artificial. Benches line the quad, along with statues and fountains, and the parking lot looks straight out of some fancy car show—every vehicle probably costs six figures. I'm quite literally the only person rolling up in a taxi, and the only reason I could afford that was because I was able to work an extra shift yesterday, and my boss gave me an advance. I would've preferred the bus, but it's a three-mile walk from the nearest bus stop to here, and while I'm up for that kind of walk any other day, I didn't want to haul all of my luggage. Moving forward, though, I'll have to because I'm still working weekends at my old job. But honestly, I can just run to the bus stop, which will help me keep in shape for tryouts.

After signing the contract to attend here, I did more research and discovered they have walk-ons for the cross country and the track team as long as I can make time, which I should be able to. I just need to get into excellent shape, more than I already am.

"Are you sure you're at the right place?" the cab driver asks as he parks the cab in front of the curb at the gated entrance. He's a younger guy with a scruffy beard and tattoos on his knuckles, and he smells of old cheese for some reason.

"Yep," I reply evasively, wondering how bad this will be if even the cab driver thinks I don't belong here.

What the hell are the people who go here going to think?

I mean, I'm trying not to judge, but I have this feeling I'm going to draw attention, and not in a positive way. Not that I give a crap. If I can survive northside, my mom and my dad, then I sure as heck can survive going to a school with a bunch of rich kids. I have to if I want to get to a better place in my life.

I slide the strap of my backpack onto my shoulder then dig my card out of my pocket to pay the driver. Once the transaction is complete, I collect my other two bags, shove open the door, and move to get out.

"Good luck," the driver says snidely as I lower my feet to the pavement.

I resist an eye roll and climb out without responding. The

moment I bump the door shut, he drives away, and I'm left standing at the gated entrance, staring up at the stairway on the other side.

I'm fairly early, so not too many people are around, but I immediately get confirmation on my original speculation that I'll draw attention.

I have a pair of sunglasses on, my hair is down in waves and swept to the side, and my gray top reaches mid-stomach. My wide-leg jeans are in style and everything, but they're also frayed at the bottom, and my platform sneakers are faded. I don't think I look bad or anything, but the people around me are dressed in nice, expensive clothes, and it's evident that I don't fit in here.

But, like I said before, I'm not backing out of this deal. So, squaring my shoulders and lifting my chin, I step onto the sidewalk and head toward the iron gate. Between the three bags I'm hauling around, I struggle to get up the stairs.

"You look like you could use some help." The upbeat voice carries a hint of amusement in it.

When I glance up to see who spoke to me, I immediately grimace.

Finn—aka, the blond guy I saw in jail—is standing a step above me, looking like some sort of Greek god with the sunlight casting across his back and creating a halo of light around him.

Great. The last thing I need is for some guy who saw me in jail to be here, talking to me. Not that I'm that surprised. Even when he was in jail, wealth flowed off this guy.

"I'm good," I assure him, resisting another eye roll when he grins at me.

I start up the stairs again, trying to look more relaxed than I feel.

The dude turns and follows me. "You don't look like you're good. In fact, you look like your legs are going to buckle." He reaches for one of my bags. "Here, just let me help."

"Hard pass, dude," I say as I sidestep him. Then I narrow my eyes. "And don't just grab my shit without me giving you permission."

Usually, when I throw attitude at someone like this, they get annoyed. Nope, Finn's smile broadens as he flashes me his pearly whites.

"All right, fair enough," he says while stuffing his hands into the pockets of his pants.

Before he can open his mouth again, I start walking up the stairs, and much to my dismay, he follows. I try to ignore him, but he's intent on running his mouth.

"You know," he says as we near the top of the stairs, "after our first meeting, I honestly thought we'd never see each other again. I guess wishes do come true."

I throw him a gaping look. "Are you for real right now?"

"What?" He bats his eyelashes innocently at me. "I'm just telling the truth. The night after we met, I made a wish on a shooting star that I'd get to see the beautiful jail girl at least one more time."

"Oh my God, please, do not call me that," I hiss under my breath.

Too many people are already staring at me. The last thing I need is for word to get out that I was in jail a handful of days ago.

"No one's going to care that you've been in jail. But if you want me to keep it a secret, I will." He gives a short pause. "Although, I'm curious why you were in there."

"Why? Because I look like someone who's never been arrested?" I reply, my voice oozing sarcasm.

He chuckles. "Yeah, there's no way I'm going to answer that question. It's like walking straight into a trap." He scratches his wrist. He's wearing a watch that looks like it costs five times as much as everything I own, if not more. "I'm honestly just curious as to why you were there."

We reach the top of the stairs, and I dig out my phone to open the map I downloaded of the school. "Why were *you* there?" I challenge, flicking a glance in his direction.

His smile is all Cheshire cat. "I'll show mine if you show me yours."

"Hard pass." I direct my attention to my phone and the map on the screen. It's overwhelming to look at, with all the paths of sidewalks, the roads, the hallways, the corridors.

"I can show you around, if you need me to," Finn offers then extends his hand toward me. "I'm Finn, by the way."

I don't take his offered hand. "I know."

A crease forms between his brows. "How do you know?"

"I heard your brother call you that while you guys were in the jail cell." I chew on my bottom lip, considering his offer.

Letting him show me around wouldn't be too awful, right?

Except, it would. I don't want him to think he could use me as a mistress or knock me up and bail. Not that I think all of them are that way, but I'm not about to risk it. Plus, I have this rule where I avoid guys in general. The last thing I want is to end up like my mother—pregnant at eighteen and dropping out of school.

"Thanks, but I'm good." Adjusting the handle of one of my bags higher onto my shoulder, I hurry forward down the sidewalk and toward the entrance. Thankfully, he takes the hint and doesn't follow me.

People continue to gawk as I climb higher, finally reaching the set of double doors. I pull one open, and hell, it's heavy. Like, what are they expecting to happen here? A tornado to blaze through? We're so in the wrong kind of area for that.

It swings shut with a loud *thud* as I step inside, and the noise carries down the spacious hallway and bounces against the domed, cathedral-like ceiling. A handful of people turn to look at me, their eyes sweeping up and down my outfit. I offer them a sugary-sweet smile, and one of the girls blasts with a nasty look, flips her long, auburn hair off her shoulder, and turns her nose into the air.

I'm getting some *Mean Girls* vibes here, but every school has them. My old school had a Mean Guys group, and they were the worst.

Turning away from the group, I make my way down the hallway until I reach the main office. It's probably the plainest of entrances, but that doesn't mean it's plain. It is a wide, arched brick doorway and above it, engraved in the brick is, *"The Main*

Office of the Royal Academy," and just above that is a golden crown carved of sparkling metal—the school crest.

Sucking in a breath, I enter through the doorway and step into the room. A handful of tables are close by, with chairs surrounding them. A few are occupied with students doing something on computers. The sounds of clicking keyboards flit through the air, but other than that, the air is silent. It's kind of unnerving and something I'm not used to since my old school was always filled with shouting, slamming, and other noises that indicated yet another fight.

Everyone appears content, though, and extremely focused—

"Can I help you?" A voice cuts through my thoughts.

When I glance at the front of the room, where a long counter is, an older woman with dark brown hair and glasses is looking at me with a curious expression.

"Um ... Hey." I hurry up to the counter. "I think I'm supposed to check in here and get a key to my dorm room. I was a late enrollment."

Again, her curiosity is evident as she glances me over, but she doesn't sound rude as she turns to the computer and asks, "What's your name, dear?"

"Maddison Averly." I set one of my bags down, my shoulder aching from the weight.

"Ah, yes, you're the scholarship student," she replies as she clicks the keys. "This is the first year the academy is allowing that, and it's a much-needed change." She offers me a smile. "I'm sure you're going to love it here, and while it might seem intimidating, don't let some of the more"—she wavers as she reaches for a booklet—"intense students scare you off. There's some nice ones here, as well."

I nod, tucking a strand of hair behind my ear. "Thanks for the advice."

She's nicer than I expected, and I'm glad. Hopefully, what she said is true. I'd like to think so, but I'm wary, considering everyone has been staring at me since I stepped out of that cab. Although, that Finn guy seemed nice enough. Flirty, but not a total asshat.

"You're welcome. I'm sure you'll be fine." She offers me a smile that makes me believe she doesn't quite believe that. Then she sets a pamphlet down. "This has a QR code that you can use to access all the information about the school that's not already online. It also has a map in case you want to go old-school. And you should now be able to access the scan code to your dorm room from your school account." She adjusts her glasses. "You do have a roommate, but the bedrooms are sepa-rated by a sitting area, and you also have your own bathroom attached to the bedroom."

I blink at her. "How big are these rooms?"

"Pretty big," she tells me then leans forward and whispers, "I grew up on the northside, too, so fair warning: everything here will seem way bigger and way more extravagant than you're used to. And you probably won't ever get used to it, but it can be a good thing. It keeps you level-headed."

I nod in agreement then collect the pamphlet. "Thanks."

"Again, you're welcome." She smiles. "Your room is in The Crystal Hallway, and you're in the Purple Crown Room."

Releasing an uneven breath, I nod, give her a small wave, then turn around and start my journey toward my room. As I walk, I unfold the map, figuring I don't mind old-school because old-school has been my life, considering the only systems my school had that were considered modern were the security cameras, and half of those didn't even work.

I like having the map open, anyway, because it gives me a distraction from all the staring and whispering. Thankfully, not many students are flooding the hallways yet, but I can tell when classes start tomorrow, my life could end up being a living hell. Not that I'll give this up. No, this is a once-in-a-lifetime opportunity—I realize that now.

Finally, after what feels like an eternity, I arrive at the Purple Crown Room—the door has a purple crown emblem on it. Music is filtering from the inside. I think it might be a Taylor Swift song. Not that I'm that familiar with her music, but it's always playing on the radio.

Tucking the map underneath my arm, I upload the scan code and put it in front of the scanner below the door handle. The door clicks unlocked and, telling myself that I've got this, even though I'm unsure if I do, I push the door open. I'm immediately blasted by the loudness of the music, along with a girl singing in the perfect pitch.

I peer around the room, wondering why I can hear but not see her.

Walking over the threshold, I kick the door shut and clutch the handles of my bags as I absorb my new home for the following year. It's bigger than the house I grew up in, with a roomy living room decorated with velvet sofas, rugs, a few end tables, and a corner fireplace. Just behind all that is a kitchen with all the fixings, including a counter area, sink, cupboard, a stove and microwave, and a table is adjacent to that. The walls are painted the prettiest shade of purple, probably to match the room's name—

"Oh my gosh, I didn't realize you were in here." The girl, who more than likely was the one singing, suddenly materialized in the doorway to my right.

She has blonde hair pulled up in a high ponytail, her eyes are smoky, her lips are lined, and she's wearing a pair of wide-legged pants and a crop top with a high neck. She's also rocking diamond earrings and a matching bracelet. Everything about her screams wealth, but what else was I expecting?

She holds up a finger. "Just a second. Let me turn the music down." She disappears back into the room. A moment later, the music turns off, shuffling follows, and then she returns to the doorway, this time walking all the way through and approaching me with her hand outstretched. "I'm guessing you're my new roommate. My name's Lillian. Everyone calls me Lily, though, and I'm so glad because my mother's name is Lillian, and it's just ... who wants to be called their mother's name, right?"

So, she's a talker. I also can't remember the last time I shook someone's hand. Not wanting to get off on the wrong foot, though, I shake her hand.

"My name's Maddison, but everyone calls me Maddy. Not because I'm named after my mom. People just started calling me that in kindergarten." I lower my hand to the side and adjust my weight as she observes me. I can tell her wheels are turning as she takes in my worn jeans, shirt, and boots, so before she can say anything, I add, "I'm a scholarship student. You can probably tell that."

"Yeah, I can, but I don't think that's a bad thing or anything like that." She tucks a loose strand of hair behind her ear while scratching her arm. "I think it's great the academy is bringing in other students besides the stuck-up snobs that go here. Not that I'm one," she quickly adds. "I promise I won't judge or anything like that. In fact, I'm excited to spend time with someone from the northside ..." She trails off, shaking her head and sighing. "Sorry, I ramble when I'm nervous. I don't do well in new social situations. I've been working on it in therapy for years, but still suck at it." She sighs again. "And now I'm oversharing again."

"Don't worry about it," I tell her. "I don't necessarily struggle in social situations, but I'm not a very social person either, so maybe we'll click."

She smiles at that, and it seems genuine. "I think we will. I can feel it." Her eyes light up. "Oh, and I can show you around if you want me to. I'm a freshman, too, but my brothers started here last year, and I would sometimes come hang out with them on weekends, so I learned where everything is—the dining hall, the library, the athlete room, the dessert room—"

"The dessert room?" I cut her off. "What the heck is that?"

She softly chuckles. "It's a room where you can order any dessert you can think of. We can go later if you want. I just need to finish unpacking."

"Yeah, I should get my stuff put away, too." I pat my bag

that's draped over my shoulder. "But I'm so curious to see this dessert room."

Excitement lights up her face and makes me question if she has any friends. She says she doesn't do well in new social situations, so there could be a possibility that she doesn't.

"Sweet—no pun intended." She laughs, and I do, too. "Your room's right there." She points to a lavender door just behind me. "It should only take me about five more—" Her eyes dart to the entrance door, and she groans. "Are you seriously coming to check on me already? We've only been here like an hour?"

"I came to make sure that all of your stuff arrived," a male voice floats over my shoulder. "And to also ensure you're aware that orientation is today."

"Yes, and yes," she replies dramatically. "I'm not incompetent."

I twist around to see who she's talking to and do a sort of dumbass double-take. But I can't help it. It's River, the guy who was in jail with Finn.

He looks marginally less intense than he did in the cell, but he's not wearing his leather jacket and almost all-black outfit. Instead, he's sporting a dark pair of pants, a gray button-up shirt with the sleeves rolled up, and a red tie.

Is this how everyone dresses here? In nice clothes? Because I'm so screwed if that's true.

Part of me wonders if he'll recognize me. After all, we only saw each other in jail. Sure, Finn did, but River didn't interact with me. But when he notes my face, he blinks twice, letting me know that he does.

"I don't think you are," River says while looking at me, but he's talking to Lily.

"Yeah, yeah, I've heard that before," Lily mumbles, then adds in a more upbeat tone, "Oh, this is my roommate, Maddy." She moves up beside me. "Or, well, Maddison, but everyone calls her Maddy. And Maddy, this is my brother, River." She gestures at him.

He eyes me over in a scrutinizing way. "Yeah, we've already met."

"Really?" she wonders. "Like in the hallway?"

"No." He stares at me for a beat longer. "When I went to northside the other night with Finn." He tears his gaze off me and focuses on Lily while massaging the back of his neck. "She gave us directions."

Ah, so that's where the nervous body movement is coming from. He doesn't want his sister to know he was in jail.

"Yeah," I play along but decide to mess with him. "He actually hit me with his car."

His attention snaps to me while Lily goes, "*What?*"

"Don't worry; it was just a little bump." I give a dismissive shrug, and he glares at me. "He bumped into me while I was stepping off the curb. It was dark, though, and it was barely a tap."

"Are you okay?" she asks me with wide eyes.

I feel bad for lying to her, but River started it. "I'm perfectly okay," I promise her. "It didn't even leave a bruise."

Her eyes remain wide as she bobs her head up and down. Then she flicks a dirty look at her brother. "You seriously need to be more careful when you're driving, River. I know you like to race, but save it for the track."

The muscle in his jaw ticks. "Okay, I'll try."

"Not *try*. *Do*," she stresses firmly. With that, she turns away from him. "One of the movers delivered a box of yours to my room by mistake. Let me grab it." She walks away and into her room.

River immediately hisses, "Why the hell did you lie to her?"

I lift my brow. "Why the hell did *you* lie to her? Because I was just rolling with your lie."

His eyes darken. "You didn't have to add the part about the car."

"And you didn't have to lie to her in the first place," I quip. "So, maybe you should just tell her the truth."

"I don't want her knowing I was in jail," he stresses while fiddling with his tie.

"Why?" I wonder curiously.

"Because," is all he says. Then he shifts his weight, giving me a once-over. "Why are you even here, anyway?"

"Why are you here?" I throw back at him.

He stares at me for a beat. "Because my father forced me to go."

"Well, I didn't get forced by anyone to go here," I tell him. "And I'm sure you can put two and two together and figure out that I'm a scholarship student, considering I'm pretty sure you overheard my conversation on the phone with my mother about my finances." I know he did because he and Finn looked at me with pity in their eyes after I was done, which is daunting right now since he appears only to be annoyed with me.

"How did you get the scholarship?" he asks. "That's not typical for here. Usually, they don't even allow that sort of thing."

His comment irks me, as if I shouldn't be allowed to go here.

"Oh, you know, I did the normal thing any northside girl does to get what she wants," I say in a sugary-sweet tone. "I slept with a bunch of rich dudes until I could convince one to pay my tuition. It was really exhausting, let me tell you, because I had to wait around for all of that Viagra to kick in."

He gives me a dumb sort of look that is so gratifying. Then, as an extra bonus, his sister returns then, so the conversation ends on that note.

"Here's your box." She presents it to him as if handing him a Christmas present.

A few items are sticking out of it. They appear to be trophies with a metal running man at the top.

Wait ... Is River a runner?

Ugh, does that mean if I make the cross-country team, I'll have to see him on a daily basis? Blah, even if he is cute. Then again, he's my roommate's brother, so crossing paths with him will be inevitable.

He frowns at the box. "I don't know why Mom thinks I need to bring my trophies to school."

"Maybe as a reminder of how awesome you are?" she suggests with a shrug.

"Doubtful," he mutters, and I sense some tension in that

statement. Shaking his head, he clears his expression and focuses on his sister. "Don't be late for orientation." He flicks a glance at me before leaving the room.

Lily huffs out a dramatic breath before turning to me. "Sorry about that. He can be so moody sometimes."

"No worries."

"Do you have any siblings?"

"No. Sometimes I wish I did, though."

"I wouldn't wish that hard," she informs me. "Okay, well, maybe having siblings isn't so bad, but having three older brothers sucks big time."

"You have *three* older brothers?" I ask with wide eyes.

She bobs her head up and down. "Yep. River, River's twin, Finn, and then I have a stepbrother, Noah, who's the same age as my brothers."

"Seriously?" I ask, and she nods. "And you're only a year younger than your brothers?"

She nods again and shifts her weight. "Things were kind of crazy when we were younger. I felt bad for our nanny."

I was my own nanny growing up, but I'm not about to share that with her.

"I bet." As the weight of my bags begins to cause my shoulder to ache, I shift my weight. "So, what's this about an orientation?"

"It's a thing we're required to go to. Basically, from what I understand, it'll be an hour of listening to the dean yammer about how amazing this academic year will be and the standards we're supposed to uphold. She'll also give information on clubs and sports."

"Really?" I perk up at that.

"Are you interested in something?"

"Cross-country and track. I had a scholarship to the Royal City Community College." I pause, debating whether to tell her I lost that, but then decide against it. She seems nice enough and everything, but I barely know her. And I have trust issues— I've known that for a while. "But then I got the scholarship here, and this is a way better school."

"Is it?" she mumbles then puts a smile back on her face. "Well, you're in luck because we have one of the best coaches in the country. River was actually on the team last year. He's been running since he was a kid." An odd look crosses her face, almost as if the memory makes her sad, but why? "But, anyway, River's on the cross country and track teams, and Finn is the quarterback for the football team. Sports here are highly competitive, but maybe I could ask one of them to give you some pointers."

"Maybe." I pause. "I think I should probably ask Finn, though."

Her head angles to the side. "Have you met him?"

I nod. "And he seems nicer than River. No offense. I know he's your brother."

"River's intense, I know. And I get that he can be an asshole, but he has it rough." She pulls a whoops face, as if she didn't mean to say that aloud. "But, if you can become his friend, he's a ride-or-die kind of person."

A ride-or-die kind of person, huh? Doesn't seem like he is, but what the heck do I know? I barely have any friends.

"Okay, I'll try to see past the assholery," I assure, but deep down, I doubt I'll be able to.

She smiles. "Awesome ... If you want to get ready for orientation, we can walk there together, if you want."

"Sounds good." I make my way over to the door that leads to my bedroom, half my mind on the idea of asking River for help and the other half stuck on what I overheard about the attire requirement for this orientation thing. Should I change? Do I even own anything nice?

My thoughts laugh at me. What am I going to wear? My nice pair of jeans?

"Holy crap," I whisper at the sight of probably the nicest room I've ever stepped foot in.

As soon as my foot steps into my new room, all my attention gets locked in on the space before me—purple and black wallpaper, a crystal chandelier, a four-poster bed decorated with an amount of velvety pillows no one in the world would ever need. The floor is partially covered with a rug, a dresser in the corner, and a fireplace is on the farthest wall. It also has a closet and bathroom.

I let my bags fall to the floor with a *thump* as I enter further and turn in a circle, taking everything in—the photos on the wall, the crown painted on the arched ceiling, and the window with a view of the land, forest, paths, and statues, along with a massive, shiny domed stadium where the track is slightly visible.

I exhale a breath as I stare out at it. I always dreamed of

running on the track team in college. I just need to make the team. I'll admit I looked up PR times for last year, and I have my work cut out of me.

I might end up getting desperate enough to ask for River's help. Whether he will or not is an entirely different story. Plus, could he even help me that much? He did have trophies in that box, but still ...

I dig out my phone and pull up the PR list online. Then I search for his name, and my jaw nearly bitch-slaps the floor.

Yep, he could help me. At least he's fast enough that he probably has some pointers.

"Good God, that's fast." I stare at his records for a while before pocketing my phone. Then I head to my bags so I can unpack.

Ten minutes later, I have everything put away, and it's clear the closet has too much space for my stuff. Still, I feel this weird sensation in my chest, almost as if I could be happy, maybe, just maybe. Then my phone buzzes, and I'm reminded that while I might have temporarily left northside, that doesn't mean it hasn't been part of me for my entire life.

Hannah: Hey, babe. I'm still on the road trip, but Will heard a rumor that Drew is looking for you and that there's a whisper put out on you. Please tell me you're okay.

I grit my teeth as I read the text. A whisper is a discreet word northside uses to let everyone know a bounty has been put on someone. It doesn't necessarily mean they're going to kill me, but it won't be pretty if they catch me. In fact, I know what they will do—they'll beat me up then probably make me either sell drugs or whore myself out to pay for what my father's done.

Suddenly, I'm even more grateful to be at the academy because, besides the people involved in my scholarship, no one else knows where I am.

I chew on my thumbnail as worry stirs inside me. What if someone does find out? I don't see how they would, but it could happen.

Just take a deep breath, Maddy. If you can get through your childhood, you can get through this.

I send Hannah a reply.

Me: I'm good. Just hiding out for a while. I'll keep you posted.

Hannah: I'm so glad. I was so worried. If you need anything, please ask. I know it's not your style, but I want to help.

I won't ask her for help because it's not my style, and it's not her style either. Hannah is wild as hell, and I'm not. To be honest, I think part of the reason we still talk to each other is because we've been friends since we were kids. We're not close anymore, haven't been since she started dating Will, who's a total wanna-be badass. It's so annoying.

"Hey." Lily pokes her head into her room, startling me. "I don't want to interrupt your unpacking or anything, but I wanted to see if maybe you needed help picking out something to wear." She crosses her arms. "I mean, you can totally wear what you have on, but I'd feel like the worst roommate ever if I didn't let you in on the unsaid dress code for these types of things. It's never required to dress a specific way to events. However, we'll be judged—we're always judged."

"Thanks for the tip." I stand up and toss my phone onto my bed. "I'm not a nice outfit sort of girl, so I don't know if I have anything, but I'll see what I can find."

I step into the closet and start sifting through the clothes that I hung up. "I have a dress," I call out. "But that's about it."

"Can I see it?"

"Sure." I exit the closet with the plaid, thin-strapped dress in my hands. It reaches just above my knees, but the top shows a lot of skin. "I'm not sure if it'll work or not."

"It's super cute, but ..." She taps her finger against her lip. "Maybe if you wore a fitted T-shirt underneath it? Do you have one?"

"I have a black one."

"That'll look so cute."

"Am I trying to look cute?"

"Cute and classy."

Her outfit does fit into those categories.

"What about tights?" she asks, assessing the dress as if she's visualizing the finished outfit.

I shake my head. "Nah, I don't own any. Never have."

"Really?" Her eyes widen as I shake my head again. She considers this then asks, "Do you want to borrow a pair of mine?"

Tights sound like an awful, itchy thing to wear, but again, I want to attempt to do well here, so I nod and tell her, "Sure. Thanks."

Her smile widens, and then she exits the room. A moment later, she returns with a pair of knee-high tights. Then she leaves so I can change.

The outfit is cute, but I feel odd, like I'm playing dress-up. So, I decide to slip my leather jacket on. While I want to fit in, I don't want to lose my identity.

I am who I am, and it's something I've always lived by.

I just hope it doesn't come back to bite me in the ass.

EIGHT

MADDISON

People are staring. It's like no one has ever taught them that staring is rude. Or maybe they just don't give a shit. I need to go back to that girl, the one who gives zero craps about anything. But this place—the shininess, the wealth, the upper class—is making me feel like I'm playing dress-up in clothes that don't fit me. It's all in my head. I know this since what I'm wearing hugs my body like it's meant for me.

"God, it's like people around here have never seen someone from northside before," I state as Lily and I walk down the hallway, heading toward the room where orientation is taking place.

"Honestly, most of them probably haven't," she informs me as she tosses a nervous glance around the room. "But they're probably staring at me just as much as you."

"Really?" I question since she looks like she belongs here.

She nods, flicking a glance toward me. "There was this incident in high school, and a lot of people who go here now were involved in it." She swallows hard but doesn't elaborate.

While I want to know what happened, with how upset she looks, I'm not about to pry.

"Is everyone here like this?" I ask as my shoes scuff against the polished floor.

"No, but a lot of them are." She pauses as she stops at the end of the hallway. It enters into a massive circular room with black and white checkerboard floors, a high-arched, cathedral-like ceiling, and walls painted with splashes of color. In the center of the room is a colossal statue of some man donning a crown, and around that are stone benches where people are sitting, laughing and chatting. "My brothers aren't," she adds as she glances at a blond guy sitting on one of the benches.

They make eye contact, and his lips kick up into a smirk.

She hurriedly looks away and shakes her head. "Let's get to the orientation room." She power-walks in the direction of a hallway just adjacent to where we're standing.

Four hallways in total branch out from the quad-like room, and this is one of the many buildings that make up the campus. It's overwhelming to think about how easily I could get lost.

Sighing at the thought, I hurry after Lily, wondering who on earth that blond guy was.

"Are you okay?" I ask as I jog up to her.

Her jaw is set tight. "I just hate that guy; that's all." She forces a smile onto her face as she spots a girl with auburn hair heading down the hallway in our direction. She has her hair down and curled at the ends, and she's wearing a black dress, fishnet tights, and an oversized army jacket. She almost looks like she's from northside except for her perfectly manicured nails and the platform designer shoes.

"Wren!" Lily waves at her. "Oh my God, I thought you wouldn't show."

"I almost didn't." Wren stops in front of us. "My parents were dead set on sending me overseas, but then they learned that the prince of East Kensford was going to attend here, and you know, they thought they'd work on getting that arranged marriage they've dreamed about since I was born."

"Wait ... arranged marriage?" I don't mean to say the question aloud—I don't even know this girl—but what the hell did she just say?

She looks at me with puzzlement etched across her features.

"Sorry," I apologize. "I'm Maddison—or, well, Maddy. I'm here on a scholarship, so I don't get how everything works here."

Her confusion deepens. "I didn't realize they were letting scholarship students in." She pulls a remorseful face. "Sorry, that probably sounded ruder than I meant it."

"You're fine," I assure her, trying to pick up on her vibe. Is she nice or mean? I can't tell.

"No, it's not fine." She sighs heavily. "Sorry, I'm just having a shitty day. My parents just dumped this whole arranged marriage idea on me right before they dropped me off here."

"Arranged marriages are kind of a thing in this social circle," Lily explains. "It's not necessarily spoken about a lot in public, but privately, things are set up by our parents. Then they send us here so that we can make these ideas happen."

"What if you don't?" I wonder, fiddling with a leather band on my wrist.

Lily and Wren trade a solemn look.

"Then you end up like Ava B." Wren is the one to answer. She scratches her wrist while peering around as if she's nervous to speak about this aloud. "Her parents sent her here so she could hit it off with this specific prince, but she fell in love with another one. When her parents found out, all her money was taken away, and rumors say that she lives on the streets of northside now."

"That could be a rumor," Lily stresses as she fiddles with a heart-shaped pendant attached to her necklace. "No one knows for sure."

"No, but I think we all know that if we don't do what our parents say, even when we're grown-ass adults, they'll cut us off. And then what? We've been raised to be dependent on them."

"Yeah, I guess." Lily's shoulders slump.

Wren sighs. "Sorry for bumming you out. I'm just having a bad morning," Wren tells her then looks at me. "So, northside, I've always wondered if parents are better over there. I mean, I know it's poverty-stricken and everything, but you guys don't have arranged marriages, right?"

I laugh, but it's humorless. "No, no arranged marriages. We have to worry more about our parents doing shit like getting in trouble with drug lords and us taking the fall."

Her brow arches. "Are you speaking from experience?"

I shrug, wondering if I'll scare them off. But Wren looks

more curious than anything else, and Lily looks shocked, her eyes wide.

"Ladies." An arm drapes over my shoulders at the same time one falls over Lily's. A split-second later, Finn pushes his way between us with a cheeky grin. "Wren, how lovely to see your bright and cheery face this morning," he teases.

With an unimpressed look, she lifts her hand and gives him the middle finger.

"You know, I'd take offense to that, but in Wren language, that basically means hello, sexy." His smirk widens as Wren's eyes narrow.

"Finn," Lily warns, slipping out from under his arm and aiming a dirty look at him. "Don't start with her."

"What? I'm just teasing her. It's our thing. Right, Wren?" he asks with a twinkle in his eyes.

Wren stares at him blankly, unamused.

Finn blows out a dramatic breath. "Fine, I'll direct my lovely energy toward someone who can appreciate it."

I expect him to walk off, but he turns to me and blinds me with his pearly whites.

"Maddison, so nice to see you again."

Great, he's learned my name.

"I think we established the first time we met that your pretty boy smile doesn't work on me."

"See? You think that's an insult"—he wags his finger at me—"but all I hear is that you think I'm pretty."

I target him with a hardy-har look, but I'll admit, I almost laugh. He's kind of funny, and maybe if I'd met him in middle school, I'd have tried to become friends with him. But I'm older now and know that'll never work. Sure, I'm attending school here, but northside and southside don't mix. We're too different.

"Finn, what're you doing?" a familiar voice floats from over my shoulder.

Finn twists around, and since his arm is still around my shoulders, I have to turn around with him.

Standing behind us is none other than River.

His dark gaze sweeps across me from head to toe, as if he's checking me out. But I doubt it since he hastily narrows his eyes on his twin brother. He likely doesn't approve of what I'm wearing.

"You're supposed to be with your team," he reminds Finn in a glacial tone.

Finn rolls his eyes but removes his arm from my shoulders. "Whatever." He glances at me. "Sorry, Dad's here to ruin our fun, but we'll pick up on this later." He winks at me then basically skips off through a doorway a few steps ahead of us where other people are wandering in.

River fixes his attention on me. "I see you decided to change. That's probably a good idea."

"And I see you decided to be the same grumpy asshole," I quip with irritation. "It might be a good idea to change that. But what do I know? I'm just northside trash who doesn't know how to dress." With that, I swiftly walk toward the doorway Finn disappeared through, crossing my fingers it's the room where orientation is happening. The moment I step foot in the room, though, I become painfully aware it isn't.

The room consists of a long table with chairs, each occupied by a guy around my age. Standing in front of the table are three men, and I can tell right away they are coaches.

"This year will be brutal, but we're going to state," the tallest one is saying as he points to a digital TV in front of him.

Crap, this is a football meeting.

Back out of the room, Maddy, before anyone sees you—

My boot squeaks against the floor, and suddenly, all eyes are on me.

"Can I help you?" the coach asks me, sounding annoyed.

Finn is sitting at the table, and a confused smile breaks across his face. Then his lips part—who knows what the guy plans to say, but thankfully, he's interrupted.

"Sorry, Coach Prescot." River appears beside me and snags a hold of the sleeve of my leather jacket. "She's new here, and I'm supposed to be showing her around, but I got distracted for a second."

"It's okay, River," the coach says while eyeing me over in annoyance. "Just make sure she understands this room is off-limits to everyone except for members of the football team, just like the sign outside there says."

Whoops. There was a sign?

River nods then tows me with him as he exits the room. The instant we get outside the room, I jerk my arm away from him.

"I didn't need you to do that," I snap, noting the sign to my right that reads, "*DO NOT ENTER UNLESS PERMITTED.*" "I can take care of myself. And besides, who the heck cares if I walk into the wrong room?"

"People here do," he assures me. "And if you want to survive being here, you'll have to learn that."

"Thanks for the tips," I reply dryly. "I'll make sure not to dress like trash, I won't walk into any rooms without permission first, I'll make sure to bow down to everyone, and I'll never be myself ever again." Rolling my eyes, I start to walk away, wondering where Lily and Wren went. Why didn't they come after me? Did I misread the potential friendship vibe from them?

When River snags a hold of the sleeve of my jacket again, I'm beyond annoyed.

"What?" I twist back around to face him with a groan. "Did I miss another rule? Did I step with the wrong foot? Did I breathe incorrectly?"

He releases my sleeve and massages the back of his neck as nervousness consumes his expression. But that dissipates as he arches a brow at me. "Are you always so defensive about everything?"

"No, I just get defensive when people insult me. Even rich guys who I'm sure are used to getting their way all the time."

"I don't get my way all the time—I never get my way," he mumbles, but I don't think he meant to say that aloud since he quickly clears his throat. "I was going to say that Lily and Wren went into the orientation room because I told them I'd get you out of there." He points to the football room. "But I also assured them that once I did, I'd walk you to orientation."

Okay, I don't have an argument for that. Still, I'm not a fan of him, considering everything else he said about me.

"And I don't think your outfits are trash," he adds, scratching his arm. "It's just that it's important to be presentable at orientation. It's why I checked to make sure Lily dressed appropriately. You can wear whatever you want to classes, but for events like orientation, there's a dress code. And you might get kicked out if you don't meet it."

"Is that a rule?"

"An unspoken one."

"Oh." I frown. "So, that's why I had to dress like a preppy girl student? Because of some unspoken rule? Personally, I don't think this is much nicer than what I was wearing before. The only difference is it's a dress."

His gaze scrolls up and down me, lingering on my legs for too long. "You look fine. I promise."

Wait ... Was he just checking me out?

I misread what he was doing the first time he looked at me like that, but this is like the second time in ten minutes.

"Okay." I tug on the hem of my dress. "Well, thanks for the heads-up, I guess."

He studies me for a beat. "You didn't even say that without being defensive."

"Hey, you don't know me, dude," I reply. "I'm not always defensive. But it does come with the territory of being from northside—it's a survival technique."

He continues to study me. The guy is intense. "That could come in useful here, too. I mean, not all the time, but ..." He wavers.

"People are going to treat me like shit because I'm from northside," I finish for him. "Yeah, I already picked up on that."

He shakes his head, wisps of his dark hair falling into his eyes. "It's not just because you're from northside. Almost everyone who goes here backstabs, betrays, and lies. It's part of the royal side."

"All right, royal boy, noted." I smile when he frowns. "What?"

"Royal boy?" he replies with zero amusement.

"What? Don't you think it's fitting?" I ask with an innocent bat of my eyelashes.

"No," he responds flatly. "And please say you're not going to keep calling me that."

I lift a shoulder. "We'll see."

He heaves a dramatic sigh but doesn't argue further. "Come on; let's get in there before orientation starts."

I nod, and we start down the hallway. And in the back of my mind, I think, *Okay, he's not so bad.* But then I realize how dangerous of a thought that is.

Are you seriously getting a crush on a royal, Maddy?

No, I can't do that because royals and north-siders don't mix. Not without something terrible happening. Like I've said, I've heard stories of what can happen, and I'm not about to become some royal's secret whore. Besides, I already made a vow not to date until I'm done with school, and I refuse to go back on that promise—ever.

NINE
MADDISON

Walking into the orientation room is almost like walking into class late, butt ass-naked and screaming at the top of your lungs. So many people stare at me that I even sneak a glance down at my outfit to make sure I didn't accidentally tuck my dress in my underwear or something.

Nope, everything looks good.

At least I'm not the only person getting openly gawked at. They're also staring at River. And whispering. There's so much whispering.

"Sorry about this," River mutters as we make our way past the dining tables that are dotting across the room.

I thought orientation would be like a pep rally or something, but we're in a dining hall type of room with tables and chairs and all sorts of breakfast-type foods.

"Why is everyone staring at you?" I whisper, trying not to squirm.

"Honestly?" he answers. "Probably because I'm walking in here with you."

And just like that, my irritation returns full force.

When he notes my expression, his lips part. "I didn't mean that like how it sounded—"

"You made it." Lily materializes with a smile on her face. "I'm so sorry we didn't stop you from entering that room. We tried to yell, but you didn't hear us."

"It's okay," I assure her. "I'm honestly confused why it was such a big deal that I walked in there, anyway. So what if it was for football players only? They were just talking."

"It's about keeping their plays a secret." River is the one to reply. He looks at me with his arms crossed. "We have one of the best teams in the country, so the coaches are adamant about keeping everything they do hush-hush."

"Finn even had to sign an NDA when he joined the team," Lily chimes in as she inches forward out of a guy's way.

"Still seems a little weird, if you ask me. And if they don't want people walking into their little boys' club room, then maybe they should try, I don't know"—I shrug—"like closing the door or something."

This gets Lily to giggle, while River gives me a tolerant look.

Look at me, making new friends.

At least Lily laughed at me.

"Come on," River says as he walks over to a few chairs at a table. "Let's go sit down so we can get through this painful orientation."

TEN

MADDISON

River nailed it when he called orientation painful. It's so dull that I get a headache. The only drop of entertainment is the whispering and gawking being thrown my way. I have a feeling that my time at this school will be extremely exhausting, but it'll be worth it.

I hope.

"So, I have a question?" I ask as Lily and I return to our dorm room.

We took off the instant orientation was over, and no one made an effort to talk to either of us. A group of guys stopped River to speak with him about cross country, and part of me wanted to stay and eavesdrop, but I decided against it. And Wren snuck out before orientation was over, muttering something about being tired of this. By "this," I assume she meant the boring droning from the dean.

"What's up?" Lily is texting on her phone but glances up at me.

"This whole staring-at-me thing going on right now"—I point at a group of people doing just that, not bothering to try to hide it—"is it because it's clear I'm from northside? And do you think they'll ever stop?"

She pockets her phone and chews on her lip as she mulls it over. "Well, I think it's partly because you can tell you're from northside—and I want to point out that you can mostly tell by how you carry yourself."

"Really?" I question dubiously. "Or is it because I'm not wearing designer clothes?"

"Not everyone wears designer clothes here. And vintage is really in. The dress you're wearing, for example."

"Okay, but how do I carry myself that makes it so obvious?"

"I don't know." She shrugs. "You look super confident, like you don't give a shit about anything, and yet you also look like you're ready for a fight, if you need to."

"Okay, fair enough." I sweep a strand of hair out of my face while processing what she just described. I guess that is how people walk around in northside. They have to, to survive.

"There's also something else," she adds warily as we stop at our door. "But I'll explain it when we enter our room." She opens the app that unlocks the door then waves it in front of the scanner. With a *beep*, the door unlocks. Then she twists the handle, pushes the door open, and walks into the room.

I follow her in, shucking off my jacket and hanging it up on a hook near the door. Then I go over to the sofa to sit down and take off my shoes. I fully plan on changing into something more comfortable then wandering around campus so I can learn where everything is.

"Let me get a snack first." Lily walks into the kitchen and begins rummaging around in the cupboards. She settles on some sort of fruit-like bowl in the fridge, digs out a fork, and shoves a mouthful into her mouth. "Okay," she says around a mouthful as she makes her way into the living room and plops down on the sofa beside me. "My brother is betrothed to this girl named Isla. She is from one of the wealthiest families in the country, and so are mine. And basically, because of that, right after River and Isla were born, my parents and her parents got together and made an agreement that when River and Isla turned twenty-one, they would get married and the two families would merge their assets and become like one big super powerful family."

I wiggle my foot out of my boot. "That's ... well, that's messed up. Seriously, I didn't realize stuff like that happened in real life."

"It does in this world. Like with Wren. And yeah, it is messed up." She takes another bite of food. "Basically, if you're the firstborn, either daughter or son in the family, you're doomed."

"So, you and your other brothers don't have to deal with this?"

"No, but we have to deal with other stuff." Her eyes suddenly widen. "Not that I think we're like the only people in this world with issues. I know there are many benefits to being wealthy, I just ... I'm sorry if I'm coming off all first-world problems on you."

"You're fine." I get my other boot off then recline back on the sofa. "Everyone has their problems."

She nods in agreement. "That's so true."

I pause. "I still don't get why you brought up River's betrothed right after I asked why everyone was staring at me. Or were they staring at him?"

"Usually, River draws attention as it is." She sets the bowl of fruit down on the table beside her. "My brother is basically like that mysterious, intense guy that every girl wants to understand, but he never lets anyone in, even with his betrothed. Usually, he keeps to himself, except for the few friends he has, which really is just Finn. And in high school, he used to let me tag along with him sometimes."

"Okay ... I'm not following you on the connection between people staring at me."

"You walked into orientation with him. Just you and him. River hasn't done that with any girl, not even Isla. In fact, the two of them barely talk, so for him to be hanging out with you ... it's weird for everyone to see. And I'm guessing there will be a bit of gossip floating around that you two might be together."

I shake my head in shock. "But we barely talked. And he annoys me, and I'm pretty sure I annoy him."

"You don't annoy him. River's just that way. Honestly, I think he might like you or he wouldn't have even talked to you." She picks up the bowl of fruit again. "Just give him a chance, okay? I'm not saying you have to date him or anything like that, but you could be friends. And if he is, he could help you get on the team."

I pull a face. "I'll try, but I still don't like people thinking we're together, especially when he's betrothed."

She stuffs a grape into her mouth. "Usually, people who are betrothed date other people during school. It's not a big deal."

"It seems depressing when you know the end game."

"Yeah, but never getting to be with someone you care about sucks, too."

"True."

She offers me a slice of apple, and I take it, popping it into my mouth.

"Do River and Isla like each other?"

"They barely talk," she repeats, stirring the fruit around in the bowl. "Isla is quiet, and so is River, which makes them pretty compliant about the whole thing. Although, River ..." She trails off, swallowing hard. "Never mind."

I want to press so damn bad, but I'd be as bad as the gossipers if I did. "I feel bad for him and her."

"Me, too." She grows silent for a moment before shaking whatever thought is haunting her mind away. Then she turns to me, smiling. "You want to get lunch or something, and then I can show you around so you know where everything is?"

"Yeah, I'd really like that. Let me just get out of this dress." I mirror her smile as I get to my feet. And it feels weird because, for the first time in my life, a lightness is spreading through me. But I should've known it wouldn't last. Because the moment I step foot into my room, I receive a text from my mother.

Mom: Where are you, Maddy? I need you.

Even a day later, I still haven't responded to my mother's text, not only because I'm still pissed off at her for stealing my money, but also I'm suspicious of her out-of-the-blue text. My mother is weak when it comes to a lot of things, and if Drew's gang is threatening her to get my location, she'll cave relatively quickly.

In a desperate attempt to seek help, I call up my aunt's disconnected number again, which is pointless. I send her an email instead, but her email address no longer exists, either.

"What the hell, Aunt Ellie?" I grumble as I lightly bang my head on the headboard in frustration.

Sure, my aunt has always been sort of a wanderer who lives by her own rules and tries not to have any responsibilities, but this is the most off the radar she's ever been.

I take out the necklace she gave me when I was a kid. I haven't worn it in a while, since it's not really my style, but holding it in my hand makes me feel closer to her. I just wish I could talk to her.

Needless to say, I barely slept last night, which is a fantastic start going into my first day of class. To try to recenter myself—and start my training—I get up when the sun is barely kissing the top of the mountains, slip on a pair of running shorts, a tank top, and sneakers, then pull my hair into a ponytail, put my earbuds in, and slip my phone carrier onto my arm. In another life, I'd have wireless ones and one of those GPS watches so that I could go sans phone. But those cost hundreds of dollars, and since I currently have about thirty dollars tucked away, that isn't even close to within my reach. Yet, it doesn't lessen my enjoyment of running.

I do some warmup stretches in my room before I head out, cranking up the music as I step outside. It's chilly, but I'll warm up quickly, so I take off, jogging down the stairs before quickening my pace as I exit through the gates and into the parking lot.

I read online that students can use the track whenever, but I want to do my first run to the bus stop so I can see how the journey will be for me when I have to go to work for my weekend shift.

My feet thud against the pavement as I run toward the exit that consists of two pillars that stretch up to a sign that glitters with the words, "*Welcome to Royal Academy*." As I run under it, I get a glimpse of the massive football stadium where guys equipped with helmets in their hands and duffel bags wander in. I guess football practice starts early.

I can't help thinking about how I accidentally went into that room the other day and how everyone made such a huge fuss about it. Even though River explained why, it's still weird. Even stranger is that, when Lily was giving me a tour of the campus yesterday, she pointed out a lot of off-limits rooms. When I asked her about it, she merely shrugged and said, "I'm not sure why. That's just how they were labeled on the campus map. And River and Finn warned me about them, too. I don't think anyone knows why students can't enter them."

We talked about that for a while and concluded that perhaps the rooms were for teacher faculty. I don't know, though; it all seems odd that a school campus would have so many secret rooms. Then again, it's a massive campus, so that could be why.

My attention shifts elsewhere the farther away from campus I get. It's so pretty up here, with the paved road lined with flourishing cherry blossoms, flowers, and trails lining the road. Not a single home is in sight, so it feels like it's just me in this world, and after living in the congestion that is northside, I feel like I can finally breathe for a moment.

As I'm rounding a corner of the road, I slam straight into something solid. For a horrifying moment, I worry I've run into a car and am about to die, but as my ass hits the ground, one of my earbuds falls out, and I hear a guy curse.

"Dammit," he grits out, sounding in pain.

I manage not to completely fall down, but my ass hurts, and so do one of my ankles.

Sitting up straight, I look in front of me and realize that the "car" I ran into is none other than the one and broody River. He has his dark hair pulled back into a small bun and is donning a pair of running shorts, a tank top, and expensive running shoes —a brand I've eyed from afar, dreaming of the day when I can finally afford a pair.

Crashing into him wouldn't be so terrible, but a ways behind him is a group of runners—all guys. And all of them are eyeing us as they approach.

It's time for me to peace out.

"Sorry about that," I apologize as I stand, wincing as I put weight on my ankle but try to shake it off.

River stands up, rubbing his elbow as if he hit it when he fell. "Are you okay?"

"Yep, totally good." I wince again as I move to step by him.

He stops me by placing a hand on my arm. "No, you're not. You're hurt."

I'm not guy crazy, but the gentleness of his touch is unfamiliar enough that my stomach flutters ever so slightly.

Goddammit, what is wrong with me?

"I just twisted my ankle." I move my arm away from his hand and let the flutters wither and die, just like they should. "I'll jog it off."

He frowns. "Are you sure? You might've sprained it. You should get it checked out."

"I've had a sprain before," I inform him, taking another step forward, ready to make a quick exit before his running buddies reach us. "I know it's not that."

He watches me as I take another step forward. "Where are you running to?"

"To the moon," I joke then take off before he can ask any more questions.

"Hey," one of the runners greets me.

He has short brown hair, the greenest eyes I've ever seen, and he's tall and lean—they all are, really.

I give him a half-ass wave then pop my earbud in and hurry off before they can speak to me further.

It's not that I'm a total bitch, but I'm not the best at socializing. Plus, back in northside, whenever I found myself on the street alone with a bunch of guys around, that was my signal to get the hell out of there. And I don't believe I should throw my rules away merely because these guys have money.

I'm not that naïve. Being rich doesn't mean people are nicer or good. And I have zero trust for most people, anyway.

As I guessed, the pain in my ankle subsides after about a minute of slow running. Then I pick up my pace, hauling down the hill that leads to the bus stop. I was planning on running slower this morning, but after the crash and fall, I'm behind schedule, and the last thing I want is to be late for class.

I manage to make it to the bus stop quickly, but going back means ascending uphill, and while I manage to keep an even, respectable pace, I make a mental note to add some hill climbs into my regimen. If I make the team, anyway.

I'll admit, I'm a bit nervous, mainly because of the stuff Lily said to me. I may get desperate enough to ask one of her brothers for help. River, maybe? I don't know. He seems so intense. But Finn is the biggest flirt, and I feel like I'd get into trouble if I created a bridge with him.

By the time I arrive back at campus, a few students are wandering around. I leave my headphones in as I make my way back to my dorm room, with plans of taking a quick shower because I stink.

"Oh, hey," Lily greets me as I enter the room.

She's rocking a silk shorts pajama set, her hair is in a bun, and she's in the kitchen, pouring herself a glass of juice.

"Hey," I reply, kicking the door shut and yanking out my earbuds. "Holy crap, I stink."

She laughs at that as she walks into the living room, where I'm leaning over to take off my shoes. "How was your run?"

"Great, actually." I unlace one of my sneakers. "The road down to the bus station is so isolated. I love it."

"Yeah, River texted me and said he ran into you on that road —like literally ran into you." She drops down on the sofa. "Is your ankle okay? He wanted me to check and see."

I glance up at her as I yank on my laces. "I'm fine. And I told him that already."

"He's a worrier." She swipes her finger across the screen of her phone. "He's always been like a protective big brother to the point of being annoying. He even does it to Finn." She pauses, mulling something over. "He is a nice guy, Maddy. I know he didn't come off that way when you first met, but he seems to like you, and I think if you gave him a chance, he could help you get onto the team and stuff."

"Maybe." I kick off my sneakers and stand up straight as I

unstrap my phone holder from my upper arm. "I just don't get why he's being nice to me, because it seems like whenever I talk to him, I'm annoying the crap out of him. Not that he's necessarily in the wrong for that. I'm kind of a smartass."

"You're not that bad," she quips with a smirk. "At least, sometimes."

I flip her the middle finger, and we both laugh.

Then I sigh heavily. "Fine, I'll go to him and see if he can give me any pointers on how to better my chances of getting onto the team."

"Good." She smiles at me as she slants back on the sofa. "Let me know how it goes. Oh, and I was told that if your ankle hurts, ice it."

I give her a salute and head into my room to grab some clean clothes so I can take a shower. The entire time, I can't stop thinking about why River is being ... nice-ish. Even though it makes me a freak, I'm suspicious of it.

Maybe I've lived on northside for too long, but from my experience, people who are nice usually want something from you.

TWELVE
MADDISON

I used to loathe the first day of school. Like I mentioned before, I never had a ton of friends, so walking into the school hallways all by myself was the equivalent of getting shoved into a locker, something that happened to me in middle school. No, I take that back. That day wasn't that awful because I got to avoid all the school drama. Right now, I wish lockers lined the shiny, overly polished hallway because then I'd shove myself into one.

I have to remind myself multiple times that I chose to attend this school.

Guys keep smirking at me, for what, who the hell knows? And don't even get me started on the girls throwing me dirty looks. Not all of them, of course, but it's enough to make me feel like I'm about to crawl out of my skin.

Thankfully, I'm a pro at the whole I-give-zero-craps attitude and manage to hold my head up high to my first class of the day. I try to keep a casual vibe for my outfit, sporting baggy jeans and a gray top that reaches just above my belly button. I have a few tattoos; one on my arm, another on my side, and the final one is on my leg, but none of them are on display. My hair is in a ponytail, and I rocked my scuffed boots. Again, it's evident I'm from northside, but what else am I supposed to do? Hide who I am? No, thanks. And I couldn't even if I wanted to.

"Hey, new girl," a guy calls out as I stroll into class, adjusting my backpack. He has blond hair and the body of a football player. He's also donning a grin as he leans over and pats the seat beside him. "I saved you a seat."

"Hard pass," I reply then veer toward an empty seat that's as far away from him as possible and plop down into it.

"Well, that was rude." Humor rings in his tone. "I saved you a seat, and you blow me off? Do you even know who I am?" His voice is growing closer, which means he's walking toward me.

I ignore him, but I'm on guard, my fingers curled into fist. If I have to hit him, I will.

"Porter, leave her alone," another voice joins the conversation, deep and male and recognizable.

I sigh. River. What is this guy's deal with me?

"Why does it matter to you?" the blond guy replies.

"That's none of your damn business," River tells him in a glacial tone. "Now go sit the hell down."

This causes me to twist around in my seat. Up until this point, I thought River was a quiet, brooding sort of guy. He has an intense side to him, too, that he likes to display.

Today, he's wearing gray pants and a black short-sleeved shirt. Like every other time I've seen him, his dark hair is dangling in his eyes. He's also standing right behind me and glaring at the blond dude, who has his hands raised in front of him and backs away.

River continues to glower until Blondie sits his ass back down. Then he turns to me with his lips parted.

"Don't ask me if I'm okay," I speak first. "I can handle assholes. I've been doing it my entire life." I twist back around in the chair.

I'm sitting in the middle row. The seats are staggered, like in a stadium, only this room is much smaller. The ceiling is high arched with beams, and bookshelves line the walls. Fitting since it's American Literature.

"I wasn't going to ask you if you were okay about Porter." River hesitates before sitting down in the chair beside me. "I was going to check and make sure your ankle is okay."

"It's fine. Your sister said you texted and asked if I was okay." I pause then add, "Thanks for checking on me."

Amusement flashes across his face.

"What?" I wonder if I have pieces of bagel stuck in my teeth or something.

"It's nothing." But his amusement suggests otherwise. He attempts to scrub his hand over his mouth in an attempt to hide it, but I see it, there and glittering.

I narrow my eyes at him as I swing my bag off my shoulder and drop it beside my feet. "Clearly, it is, or you wouldn't be smiling like that."

He lowers his hand from his mouth and rests his arms on the table in front of us. "Fine, it's just that you said thanks."

"And ...?"

He shrugs. "And it was almost like you were getting your teeth pulled."

Okay, it's frightening how on-point he is. Still ... "I say sorry on occasion."

"Okay."

"I do," I insist defensively.

"And I said okay." He's on the verge of smiling again.

"You know, when I first met you, back in that place we're both pretending we weren't at, I got the impression that you were the quiet, brooding type, but I misread you." I lean over to dig a pen and notebook out of my bag. By the time I sit up, his smile has faded. I heave a dramatic sigh. "What did I say now?"

"Nothing." He falls silent. I've struck a nerve, yet I'm not sure if it was the subtle mention of us being in jail or my remark about him being quiet and brooding. And I shouldn't care. I've never cared about a guy before. But I told Lily I'd try.

He remains silent as he unzips his leather bag and pulls out a laptop.

I realize everyone else has one out, as well. Why I didn't think of that is beyond me. I have one back in my dorm. It's old and worn, but at least it's functional.

"Crap, I forgot my computer," I mumble then move to stand up.

He snags a hold of the hem of my shirt, his fingers grazing my flesh.

If I thought I felt butterflies when he touched my arm after we crashed into each other, I was wrong. Because holy fluttering monarchs, does my stomach erupt with flutters to the point where I startle.

"Sorry." He quickly jerks back.

"You're fine." I think.

I don't know ...

What the hell was that?

"Sorry," he replies again, in a much more even tone. "I was just going to say that if you're late to this class, Professor Madella will make a big deal about it in front of everyone."

Grimacing, I lower back down into the chair. "That's the last thing I want."

"I assumed so."

"Why?"

He lifts a shoulder. "You just seem like the type who doesn't like to draw attention, even though you do." He stares down at the keyboard of his laptop.

"Yeah, I know. I reek of northside, don't I?" I sink back into the chair with a heavy sigh.

"No, that's not it." He avoids eye contact with me as he boots up his laptop.

"What is it, then?" I question then add dryly, "My charming personality?"

He rubs his lips together, on the verge of smiling again. "You say that like you're joking, but it's kind of true."

I put the end of my pen to my lip. "Only kind of, huh?"

His smile breaks through, but he hastily wipes it away as a guy with brown hair steps up in front of us and clears his throat.

He's cute with full lips and the greenest eyes I've ever seen. He also seems vaguely familiar.

"I hate to break up this little moment, but I need the keys to the car. I left my bag in the trunk the other day." He sneaks a curious glance in my direction.

It takes me a moment to connect where I've seen him—he was the guy who waved at me while I was running.

River pats his pockets then fishes out a set of keys. "Just make sure to lock it up." All of his humor is gone. He's not rude or anything like that; merely guarded.

The guy offers him a tense smile then looks at me. "You're the new girl, right?"

"The one and only," I tell him. "I prefer to be called Maddy, though, not new girl."

"I'll make a mental note of that." He starts down the aisle. "I'm Noah, but I'm sure you've already heard of me." He doesn't wait for me to respond as he exits the classroom.

"That's your stepbrother," I state as the name clicks.

"Yep," he mutters while staring down at his hands.

I sense some tension there. "You two don't get along?"

"We're just not friends." He slants back in his chair, crosses his arms, and stares straight ahead. And there's the broody, quiet guy whom I first saw in jail.

I decide to let the conversation drop, but I'm curious what's behind the tension. My best bet is the fact that Noah's mom had an affair with River, Finn, and Lily's dad, which led to the divorce and remarriage.

As we sink into silence, I note a girl at the bottom of the

aisle staring at me. She has long, blonde hair in braids, her makeup is minimal but flawless, and her fitted green sweater and wide, pin-striped pants look fashionable. Her gaze slides between me and River, and her brows furrow.

"Um, so I hate to break up your little solo brooding moment, but who is that girl staring at us?" I give a subtle nod in her direction.

He tracks the nod, and his frown deepens as he hastily looks away. "That's Isla."

"Oh, the betrothed." The words slip out of my mouth before I can stop them. "Shit, sorry. That was probably insensitive."

His gaze shifts to me. "Lily told you?"

I tap my pen against the desk. "Only because I was asking her all these questions about why everyone was staring at me during orientation. I thought it was because I was from northside—and honestly, I'm still convinced that's part of it—but then she told me about the"—I gesture at the front of the classroom where Isla is—"well, you know." I feel awful, considering the moroseness that's consumed his features. "Sorry for bringing it up. I like to do this thing sometimes where I put my foot in my mouth. It's a real friend magnet, let me tell you."

His eyes scroll over me. "You're not that bad."

"Only somewhat bad," I quip, to which he responds with an attempt at stifling a smile. I fiddle with the cap on my pen, sliding it off and on. "So, I have a subject change I'm going to offer right now to slide on right by this." I set the pen down to stop my fidgeting. I'm not even positive why I'm doing it. Okay, that's a lie. I know exactly why—because I'm about to ask for a favor.

He absentmindedly rotates a ring on his finger. "Okay, what is it?"

"It's a favor," I start then hastily tact on, "And you can totally say no. Your sister suggested that I ask you—or, well, she said I could ask you, Finn, or Noah, because you're all on sports teams." And ... I'm rambling. "But, anyway, I want to get onto the cross country team, and Lily said it was hard to navigate the sports world at the academy. So, if you could offer me some pointers on navigating it all, that'd be so helpful." I give him a cheeky grin at the end of my speech, hoping that'll entice him even more.

He blinks at me then stares like I sprouted a unicorn horn out of my ass. "You're asking me about sports?"

"Um ... yeah?" I grow a bit twitchy. "You don't have to if you don't want to. In fact, forget I asked."

"No, it's not that." He shakes his head and blinks again. "Sorry, it's just that when someone asks for a favor, it's usually something much bigger than me giving pointers."

"I can actually understand that." I chew on my bottom lip. "I mean, I'm sure you heard my convo with my mother on the phone, back when ... well, you know."

Discomfort radiates from him. "I did hear a little," he confesses. "Finn did, too. We didn't eavesdrop on purpose or anything like that. It's just that—"

"We were in a confined space," I finish for him, whispering.

"You don't have to explain why. I know I was being an asshole back when we were in there, but I was having a shitty night."

His eyes search mine. "Why were you in there?"

"Why were *you* in there?" I throw back at him. When reluctance flashes across his face, I add, "How about I show you mine when you show me yours?"

A strange look rises on his expression. My bet is his mind went to a dirty place from the words I uttered, but all he says is, "Fair enough."

He begins rotating the ring around his finger again and fixes his attention on the front of the room as an older woman with short dark hair, wearing a striped pantsuit, enters the classroom. She marches straight up the podium, sets her briefcase down, and focuses on the room.

"Welcome to American Literature," she begins, her firm tone jarring for such an early hour in the morning. "The first thing you should know about my class is ..." Her words fade as a student hurries into the room.

"Sorry," he mumbles as he makes a beeline for an open seat while clutching a laptop.

"Well"—the professor looks at the classroom again—"I was just about to give my rules on being tardy for my class. However, since this young man has decided to do just that, let me make an example of what will happen if you're late." She strolls out from behind the podium and approaches the guy. "What's your name?"

He shifts in his desk. "Sebastian."

"Well, Sebastian"—she stops in front of him—"let's give the class a demonstration on why not to be tardy, shall we?"

RIVER WAS RIGHT. I don't ever want to be tardy to this class. After putting Sebastian on the spot, she proceeded to ask him all sorts of questions about American Literature, why he made the poor life choice to be late, and why he'll never be late again. I actually experienced some secondhand embarrassment from him.

"Thanks for the heads-up on not being late to this class," I tell River as I stuff my notebook and pen into my bag.

I have about an hour between this class and my next, and I have plans to return to my dorm room to grab my laptop and give my hand a break with the writing.

He slings his bag over his shoulder. "No problem. I gave Lily a heads-up about this before she came here. This school is ..." He wavers. "Well, a lot about it sucks, but the classes are excellent. Tough, but if you're looking for the best education, it's worth the toughness ... Sometimes, anyway."

"It's worth it to me; trust me. I was supposed to go to the community college," I say as we make our way out of the aisle and toward the exit. "I had a scholarship and everything, but that lovely little incident when we first met led to that getting revoked. But I lucked out when I got one here."

I expect him to ask me how I got one here, but he just says,

"What was your scholarship for at the community college? If you don't mind me asking."

"You're fine." I do my best to disregard all the staring that happens the instant we step foot into the hallway. "It was for cross country, track, and my excellent academics." I throw him a grin because, while the scholarship did get revoked, I had to kick ass to obtain it.

His brows shoot upward. "Really?"

I nod, slipping the heavy bag higher onto my shoulder. "Yeah, really." I playfully nudge him with my shoulder. "You don't need to seem so surprised about it. North-siders can kick butt, too."

"I'm not surprised because you're a north-sider," he explains as he stuffs his hands into his pockets while sneaking a glance around at the people nearby. A frown pulls at his lips, but it fades when he returns his attention to me. "It's just that getting a scholarship like that is difficult. I know because I got one here. They actually don't give out money for that due to the fact that, well, you know."

"Almost everyone here has money."

"Yeah. But, anyway, it gave me a secured spot on the team because, like Lily said, it's hard as hell to get on any athletic team at the academy. And honestly, when you asked me to give you some pointers on how to get onto the team, I assumed you were just a normal runner who wanted to make the team. So, the surprise comes from the fact that you're clearly not the average runner."

"If I was, I probably wouldn't have asked you." I inch closer to him to move around a group of guys loitering in the hallway. "I've read all the info on the website, and I could tell it was going to be a pain to get on the team. Not impossible, but I'm definitely going to have to up my training until tryouts, which is in a few weeks, right?"

He nods, slowing to a stop in front of an arched doorway that appears to lead to another hallway. "I have class this way, and I have to hurry because I need to talk to the professor before class starts, but I'd be more than happy to help you. Just get my number from Lily and text me a bit later today, and we can meet up somewhere and go over stuff."

I'll admit, I'm a bit excited about this. Although, being who I am, a trace of suspicion resides inside me as to why he's so willing to help me.

"Awesome." I start to back away from him. "You know, when I first saw you, I thought you were going to be a total douche. And when we first met, I thought, *Yep, nailed it*. But you're not so bad." I smile so he knows I'm playing.

Well, sort of.

He sinks his teeth into his bottom lip, as if biting back a smile. "Gee, thanks."

"You're welcome." I wink at him then spin around, feeling lighter than I have in a long time.

Of course, as I'm heading back to my room, my phone rings with an incoming call from my mother, which sends me into a mood dive.

"No," I mutter, silencing her call. "I won't let her ruin this for me."

She calls me again as I'm entering the my room. This time, I allow it to go to voicemail on its own as I kick the door shut behind me.

Lily isn't back yet, so I get a cup of water before heading to my room. I brought a few snacks with me when I moved in, and I mostly plan on eating in the cafeteria for breakfast, lunch, and dinner since my scholarship covers that, but I need to pick up more snacks when I head into town to work this weekend, particularly ones that have high protein in them. Although, those are generally expensive.

What I need is a better, closer job, but that would mean having to apply to jobs in Royal City, and I highly doubt I'll get hired for those—

Ping.

Apparently, my mother left me a voicemail. I have no desire to listen to another one from her. However, I must be a glutton for punishment since I press *play*, anyway, as I flop down onto my bed.

"Hey, sweetie," she says. *"I was just calling to see where you are. I'd like to get together soon and talk about some stuff. I think you might be ignoring me, and I'm guessing it's because I borrowed that money, but honey, I needed it for bills. You shouldn't have ever hid it from me. And you got out of jail, anyway, so I don't get what the big deal is."* She sighs. *"Can you please call me back? Maybe we can get together after you work on Friday? You're still working Friday shifts, right? Let me know. Love you."*

My fingers curl around the phone for some many different

reasons, one being how she blamed me for her taking my money. But that's not the worst part. No, the worst part is the giant red flag laced in her words—her eagerness to know if I work on Friday.

I'm not positive, but either she wants to make a sporadic visit to blindside me, or she's attempting to get my location for someone else, like Drew and his gang.

"Shit." I sit up and press the heel of my hand to my forehead as my mind begins to spin.

Not a ton of people are aware that I work at that café, so I wasn't too concerned about going to work. Now, I'm freaking the hell out, because I have to work. But if I go, I could end up getting caught by Drew and his friend, and then what? I don't know for certain, but it won't be good.

The only silver lining is that my boss already let me switch my schedule to Saturday and Sunday, something my mother isn't aware of. Still, I need to look into getting another job.

Shaking my head, I lie back down on my bed and stare up at the pretty ceiling. Everything is so beautiful, pristine, and nice, to the point of near perfect. Light, that's what I think of when I look around at my surroundings. And yet, my life is clouded with darkness, proof that I can take myself out of northside, but I can't take northside out of myself, even if I desperately want to.

THIRTEEN
MADDISON

I feel defeated for the rest of the day. Like broke-the-hell-down-on-the-side-of-the-road-with-no-money-in-the-rain-with-a-stalker-lurking-the-bushes kind of broke the hell down.

I'm an expert at feeling like this, so I manage to get through my other class for the day. But then I return to my dorm with a plan on grabbing my snacks, locking myself in the room, and cranking up the most depressing music I can find. So, basically, just going all emo. When I enter the dorm, however, Wren and Lily are lounging on the sofa, chatting about classes and tryouts for something.

"Hey, girl," Lily greets me as I walk in and bump the door shut. "I heard a rumor about you today."

"I heard it, too," Wren states with her attention glued to her phone. "It was juicy gossip, too, and if I didn't know you, I'd probably blog about it."

"You blog?" I ask as I drop my bag, and it hits the floor with a heavy *thud*.

"She does. And she has a whole gossip column called 'The Crown News.'" Lily has her knees tucked under her as she faces me. "Some magazine companies have even tried to get her to sell out, but my girl is all about being indie."

"I don't want any restrictions on what I write." She starts texting on her phone. "Plus, just for the record, the only reason I got offered any jobs is because my mother is one of the editors at *Glittering and Royal Magazine*, so it's really not that impressive."

"Don't sell yourself short, babe," Lily says as she puts her hair into a high ponytail. "You're an amazing writer and collector of all gossip here."

Wren shrugs, her fingers moving across the screen. "Am I?"

Lily frowns at her friend, but Wren is too distracted by her phone to notice.

I slump down in a chair. "What was the gossip you heard about me?"

Wren pushes a few more buttons. "That you and River were seen vibing in class today."

Lily stretches her legs out. "I heard it was in the hallway."

They both then look at me.

"We weren't vibing," I clarify. "We just talked."

"During class?" Wren asks.

"No, before and after. And then in the hallway for like two minutes." I sigh as I lean back in the chair and rest my head back, staring up at the ceiling. "I know he's betrothed and everything. We were just talking, so I don't get why everyone's making a big deal of it."

"Because River rarely talks to anyone." Wren is the one to answer. "So, seeing him talking to you is like seeing a unicorn."

"Unicorns aren't real," Lily tells Wren.

"I used to believe that, but if River's talking to Maddy, then who knows, maybe they are," Wren replies. "Besides, I said *like*, not that it *is*."

"You say potato. I say potatoe." Lily smirks at Wren as she narrows her eyes.

Wren sighs as she puts her phone away. "Speaking of unicorns, did you see that Penelope was here today?"

Lily nods. "Oh yeah, I couldn't miss that."

"Who's Penelope?" I intervene, feeling so out of the loop my mind is spinning.

Lily rotates to face me, her face bursting with excitement. "She's Penelope Morelis. You know, the famous actress."

My eyes widen. "What? She goes to this school?"

"She does now. She enrolled as a junior. It's crazy, right?" Wren says, and I nod, my mind spinning at this wild world I'm currently a blip in. Wren rises then and pockets her phone. "You want to drive to the city and get dinner before we hit up the party?" she asks Lily.

Lily stands up, nodding. "Yes, I'm starving,"

"What party?" I ask.

"It's the start of the school year party. The royal fraternity and sorority throw one every year," Lily explains as her gaze scans the floor. "At least, that's what Finn and River have told me. They also told me I shouldn't go." She rolls her eyes. "Sometimes, having two big brothers is beyond annoying."

I stretch my legs out and rotate my ankle, the muscles a bit tight. "You have three, though."

She presses her lips together and trades a look with Wren. "Noah doesn't really play the big brother role with me."

"Oh." I study her, recalling my brief meeting with Noah while I was with River and how their interaction was flowing with so much discomfort I could feel it.

"But, anyway"—Wren clears her throat and throws me a look I can't quite comprehend—"dinner before we hit up this little shindig?"

"Yep. Let me get changed, grab my bag, and then we can go." Lily whisks herself into her room, kicking the door shut behind her.

Wren immediately looks at me. "Just a little warning," she whispers, "I wouldn't mention Noah to any of the Averson siblings. There's a lot of messed-up history there."

"I kind of gathered that already," I tell her. "I'll try to be more careful when mentioning his name."

She sits down on the armrest of the sofa. "It's not as bad with Lily, but Finn and River were best friends with Noah since grade school, but then Noah's mom had an affair with their dad, which led to the divorce from their mom. And now Noah's mom, and they're so ..."

So, it is what I suspected. However, I didn't gather that River and Noah used to be BFFs with each other.

"That's kind of messed up," I say.

"For sure, but that's the royal world for you." Wren briefly hesitates. "Is it like this over on the northside?"

I shake my head. "No, but we have our own set of problems —drugs, gangs, violence ..."

I expect her to look horrified by what I said, but she doesn't.

"We have that here, too. I'm not sure if it's the same as in northside, but we have drugs, cliques, and violence. It just gets covered up here."

"It gets covered up on northside, too." I almost tell her about the two times I was arrested and how it wasn't my fault, but I stop myself. I don't know this girl well, and while she seems nice enough, giving out all of my secrets to her—especially when she runs a gossip column—doesn't seem like the best idea.

We fall silent as she receives a text and digs her phone out to check it. I decide to get up and change into sweatpants and a T-shirt, wanting to spend the night doing homework.

"I think I'm going to go work on some assignments."

She glances up from her phone. "You're not coming to dinner with us?"

I shake my head as the door to Lily's room swings open. "Nah. I have too much work to do."

Lily steps into the doorway. "No, you have to come. I want to get to know my new roommate."

She's wearing a blue dress, plaid jacket, and strappy heels. Wren wears black silk pants, a white shirt, and a leather jacket. Both of them are dressed fancy, at least to my standards. I can put two and two together and guess they're probably going to a restaurant where food costs more than rent back on northside.

"I wish I could, but I need to do some assignments." I pick up my shoes and start toward my room.

"Oh, come on," Lily whines as she hurries after me. "Half the fun of being in college is that we don't have to live by the standards of when we were in high school. We can go out and have fun any day we want. Plus, we have that party to go to."

"I wasn't invited," I point out.

"Everyone's invited." She grabs my arm and starts to beg. "Please, please, pretty please."

It sucks so bad because I believe she's being genuinely nice, and I would love to go and make friends with her, but I can't. Like, literally can't afford to go. And it sucks.

"How about this? You guys go get some dinner while I do my homework, and then we can meet up after, and I'll go to the party with you," I offer, hoping she'll take it. Otherwise, I might be persuaded to do something stupid. And by stupid, I mean go to a restaurant that I can't afford and end up staring at them while they eat

Can you say awkward?

"That sounds like a fantastic plan," Wren intervenes, giving me this look that has me questioning if she perhaps knows about my dilemma. She stands to her feet and urges Lily toward the door. "Let's go before we don't have time to eat."

"Oh, fine." Sighing, Lily trudges toward the door, collecting her purse. "But you swear you'll come to the party?"

I nod and draw an X across my heart. "Cross my heart and hope to die."

She chuckles as she reaches for the door handle. "We'll stop by when we're done so we can go to the party together. And no getting out of that," she playful warns as she pulls open the door.

"She's not going to get out of it." Wren gently pushes her out of the door. "Now, come. Let the new girl get her homework done." With that, Wren grabs the door handle and starts to pull the door shut.

When she smiles at me, I find myself mouthing, "*Thanks.*"

"*No problem,*" she mouths in return then closes the door.

I slump back into the sofa and release an exhausted noise that matches how I feel inside.

Day two here, and I'm already feeling the social class difference, but I knew this coming in and chose to be here.

That's what I have to keep reminding myself of.

Since I actually don't have much in the line of homework and need to eat, I get up, grab my phone, and head out of my room, toward the cafeteria. The place is empty, but the food, as I have learned, is wonderful. Like restaurant quality. I decide on pasta and garlic bread, grab a drink, and take my food with me as I wander back toward my room.

"You know, I think you might be the only person in this school who uses the cafeteria for dinner." Finn falls into step beside me as I'm going through one of the quads.

"And your point is?" I question with an arch of my brow.

"There wasn't really a point." He stuffs his hands into his pockets and offers me what some girls probably think is a charming smile. "I was just trying to make small talk."

"I bet you do that a lot."

"What? Make small talk?"

"No, don't have a point when you talk." I bite back a smirk when his lips part in shock.

Then his shock morphs into a sputtering laugh. "You know, you're probably right. I really do have a lot of pointless conversations." He studies me as we veer down the hallway to my dorm room, tapping his lip with his finger. "I don't think I've ever had anyone be such a smartass to me. It's kind of refreshing."

We reach my dorm room then and come to a stop.

"You think my smartass-ness is refreshing?" I cock a brow at him as I attempt to balance my food in one hand so I can dig my phone out of my pocket.

"I do ... Here, let me help." He takes the plate and drink from me before I can protest. "Most of the people who go here are fake—*plastic*. And what makes it even worse is that because of our last name, so many people kiss our asses. Not that I'm complaining that I have it that bad. I get my entitlement." He grins at me.

"I never said anything about that." But I was thinking it.

"You were thinking it, though," he says, like he can read minds.

I hate that he can, at least with me. Typically, I'm not an open book, but more like a locked journal stuffed under floorboards, underneath a bed, in a dungeon.

His smile widens. "And now you're wondering if I can read minds."

I roll my eyes but have to bite back a smile. "That's not what I was thinking."

"Liar," he teases as I scan my code and the door beeps open.

"Maybe I am a liar. Maybe not." I take my plate and cup from him. "You'll probably never figure it out."

"Actually, I don't think you're a liar. In fact, I think you might be the most honest person I know."

"I'm really not."

"We'll see," is all he says.

Resisting another eye roll and potential smile, I step over the threshold and into my room, lifting my foot to kick the door shut. But he places his hand against it, stopping me.

"I actually have a question for you."

"Okay, you can ask it, but I won't promise I'll answer." I set my food and drink down and turn to face him. "What's up?"

His gaze sweeps across the room, and then his brows knit. "Wait—you're rooming with my sister?"

"Is that your question?"

"No, I just realized her stuff is in here."

"Oh. Well, yeah, I am. Why else do you think we were going to orientation together yesterday?"

He shrugs. "I just thought maybe you guys made friends."

I waver. "Please don't take this the wrong way, because I think your sister's really nice, but I don't think we would've even talked to each other had we not been roommates."

He drags his teeth along his bottom lip. "I don't know. It's not that surprising to me. Sure, you guys seem like opposites—although I barely know you." A smile creeps onto his face again. "Well, other than you're a smartass, which Lily isn't. Still, I get the whole social outcast vibe coming off you, and Lily can be like that sometimes. Or, well, she has in the past." He pulls a whoops face. "Please don't repeat that."

I snort a laugh. "Who would I tell? I haven't talked to anyone besides Lily, Wren, you, River, and Noah." I set my phone down beside my food. "Besides, it's not my thing to gossip."

"I wouldn't guess it was. In fact, you seem like you're the opposite ..." He trails off. "Wait, you talk to Noah?"

"For like five seconds." I pick up one of my slices of garlic bread and pop a chunk into my mouth. "And only because I was talking to River, and he came to talk to him, so he introduced himself."

That seems to astonish him even more. "You were talking to River?"

"I just said I was. And you saw me the other day while I was."

"But that's not the time you're referencing."

"Well, no. I'm talking about while I was in my first class today."

His shock magnifies. "So, you've talked to my brother twice already?"

"Yeah, so?" I shove another bite of bread into my mouth. "Why is everyone making such a big deal about this? I get his whole betrothed thing, but so what if we talked? Is he not allowed to talk, either?"

"No, he's allowed to. He just doesn't do it very often." He leans against the doorjamb with his arms crossed. "You saw him in that jail cell, all silent and brooding. Well, that's pretty much how he is twenty-four seven. He must like you or something."

"He barely knows me, so I doubt it."

"You don't seem too impressed that he might."

I smile cheekily. "Should I swoon, like I did over you in jail? Oh, wait, I did not do that, even though you tried to get me to."

He drags his hand across his mouth to conceal a smile. "Hell, you're entertaining." He lowers his hand to his side. "We have to be friends."

I cross my arms. "Friends, huh? Why do I get the feeling you don't have female friends?"

"Hey, that's not true at all."

"Really? Or are you including friends with benefits?"

He squirms ever so slightly. "Okay, maybe that's partially true. But I don't screw every woman I talk to." His squirminess shifts in the blink of an eye. "Besides, there's a first for every-thing, right?" He dazzles me with a grin.

And for a moment, it works on me, as my heart flutters inside my chest. But seriously, what the hell?

Stop that, you dumbass heart. You have one job, and that's to keep me alive. Not swoon.

I shake the feeling off to the best of my ability. "I guess."

"So, what do you say?" He legit sticks out his hand. "Friends?"

Do I want to try to be friends with him and his pretty boy looks and charm? Sure, having as many friends as possible would be nice, but Finn's flirty vibe could become a problem.

I keep my hands at my side. "Only if you promise not to flirt with me."

His head bobs back as he lets out a groan. "Come on, Maddison. It's like my natural personality to flirt."

At least he's being honest, I guess.

"But I'll try to tone it down with you," he adds with his hand still outstretched.

I eye his hand. Do I dare to do it? Because it kind of feels like I'm about to make a deal with the devil. A cute devil, albeit. But still, it could be a problem.

He juts out his lip. "Pretty please?"

"Oh, whatever." I shake his hand. "Let's be friends, Finn."

"It's a deal, Maddison." He pauses. "What's your last name, anyway?"

"It's Averly. And if you're going to be my friend, call me Maddy."

"Maddy?" he muses. "That's cute."

I point a finger at him. "And you're already flirting."

"I'm just complimenting your name." He flashes me his pearly whites as he removes his hand from mine. "So, new friend of mine, you're going to the party tonight, right?"

I nod. "I have to since I promised your sister I'd go with her."

"Good. I'll introduce you to some people." He backs toward the doorway. "That way, you won't have to spend this year being a loner."

"Hey, maybe I like being a loner."

"Do you?"

"Sometimes." I think. Truthfully, I don't know any other way regarding life.

Sure, I have friends, but when you have my trust issues and grew up in a sketchy environment like I did, you get used to keeping your guard up.

"You sound just like River," he remarks as he steps into the hallway. "No wonder he's been talking to you."

I lightly touch my chest. "Aw, and I thought it was because of my charming personality." My tone oozes with sarcasm.

He smiles. "It's probably a little bit of that, too." He falls silent for a second, studying me, an indecipherable look crossing his face. But he promptly erases it, his signature smile returning. "See you at the party, Maddy." He winks at me before spinning around and strolling off down the hallway.

I close the door behind me, wondering what on earth I've gotten myself into, making a promise to be friends with the popular, beautiful star quarterback.

One day at this school, and I feel like I've already become someone else.

And I'm not sure if I hate it or like it.

I spent the next hour eating and working on a few assignments. Then, once I'm done, I look more into who bailed me out of jail. It's something that's been bugging me since I was released, and while no one at the police department has handed over the information, I'm not about to stop trying. I also need to call and find out when my court date is for the charges filed against me, but it's too late to call about that. On top of all of this, I need to look for a new job. So, I guess staying here instead of going to dinner was a good thing since my to-do list is way longer than I anticipated.

I start with looking for a job online, mainly sticking to waitressing positions on the northside. Once I've submitted a few applications for those, I begin a search on anonymous bailers to see if anything pops up.

After reading article after article, I arrive at the conclusion that the person who bailed me out either bribed the police department to refuse to give me their information—which isn't legal, but this is northside we're talking about—or the person didn't give their information when they paid my bail.

But seriously, who the hell would do this? Why go through the trouble of remaining so discreet? It doesn't make any sense.

None of this does really—

Ding.

A text comes through, and I have my earbuds in, so I startle.

Releasing a shaky breath, I pick up my phone, and my brows furrow at the unrecognizable number. When I open the message, my confusion dwindles.

Hey, it's me, Lily. I meant to exchange numbers with you earlier but totally spaced out, so I called the school and got it. Sorry if that's weird, but I wanted to let you know that Wren and I will be there in like half an hour, and then we can head to the party!

I prop up on my arms as I stare at the screen. I don't feel like attending this party for so many reasons, but blowing her off is a bitch move.

Me: Okay, I'll get ready then.

I program her number into my phone and, a second later, she texts me again.

Lily: Awesome! We'll have so much fun. I promise.

I want to believe her, but I can be naturally pessimistic when it comes to parties, perhaps because the ones my parents always threw were an absolute shitshow.

Pushing up, I climb off the bed and begin rummaging through my clothes. For an instant, I consider texting Lily to see what I should wear, but I'm getting tired of worrying about that. It's not who I am, and I don't want to lose myself in this place. So, I pull on a pair of fishnet tights, a short, black skirt, and a worn Nirvana T-shirt I found at a secondhand store. Then I slip on my leather jacket, my boots, and pull my hair into a messy ponytail. I put on my dark eyeliner and mascara, and since it's a party, I add some maroon lipstick to the mix.

I call it good, and it only took me about twenty minutes, so I wander into the living room area and sink onto the sofa to wait for Lily and Wren.

I'm a mixture of nervousness—which I hate—and exhaustion—which is normal. But a tiny, tiny part of me is curious to see what party life as a royal will be like.

I sit on the sofa and scroll through my social media accounts for about ten or so minutes before the door opens up.

"I know. He's so hot," Wren is saying as her and Lily walk into the room. "Maybe I could persuade him into making out with me for a bit tonight?"

"You shouldn't have to persuade anyone to make out with you," Lily informs her as she shuts the door.

"Maybe. But couldn't I just lower my self-worth for one night?" she asks. "Is it really that big of a deal?"

"I don't think ..." Lily trails off as her gaze finds me. Then her eyes go huge. "Holy crap, you look like Grunge Barbie."

"Hey, so do not," I protest, rising to my feet. "I don't even have blonde hair."

"Not all Barbies have blonde hair," Lily comments while eyeing me over. "Man, I so wish I could pull off the grunge look."

"You can do whatever you want," Wren tells her while assessing me. "And so can you. But I feel like I should warn you that if you go to the party tonight dressed like that, you'll be treated like fresh meat."

"Thanks for the warning, but I can handle my own." I stand up, tugging at the hem of my skirt. "I need to be me. It's important."

Wren nods. "I can respect that. And I don't think it will necessarily be a bad thing. I just think you'll be hit on a lot, because you're new and different."

"And hot," Lily adds with a shake of her head. "Man, I wish I could pull off that look."

I turn toward her. "Who says you can't?"

"My pasty skin and blonde hair." Her shoulders slump as she sighs. "Whenever I've tried the all-dark vibe, it washes me out. Whatever. I'll put on a boring pastel dress or something," she mumbles then goes into her room and shuts the door behind her.

"Now I just feel bad," I mumble, tugging at the hem of my skirt.

Wren laughs under her breath. "Don't feel bad. That's just how Lily is—overdramatic about everything. But she's loyal as hell, even to a fault almost." She sits down on the armrest of a nearby chair and considers something. "Can I ask you kind of a personal question?"

"Um … sure." I retake a seat on the sofa. "I mean, you can ask, and I'll decide if I want to answer."

"Okay." She mulls something over. "How did you get the scholarship here? It's been driving me crazy, because Royal Academy has never, ever allowed scholarship students in before, but then they suddenly decide to this year, and you're the only one who gets accepted? It's just driving me crazy." She briefly pauses. "Not that I'm saying it's a bad thing. I wish they'd let more in. It's just my journalist side has been trying to piece together the whys behind it." She crosses her legs as she rotates toward me. "This school has a history of doing suspicious things —dusting shit under the rug, doing coverups for assaults and hazing—and my goal as a writer is to bring to light some of these dark secrets they're trying to hide."

"Aren't you worried that might get you into trouble?"

"Oh, I know it will. But it kind of comes with my job. And yeah, I get that I don't have to write about it, but I want to." She heaves a weighted sigh. "Despite what my parents want me to do, I don't want to spend the rest of my life being a gossip columnist. I want to write about things that matter, and I want to start with this school and its corruption."

"And you think my scholarship has to do with that?" I question, unsure whether to be offended or not.

"Truthfully, I don't know. All I know is that it's completely out of the ordinary for them to let northside students in on scholarship, especially when this place prides itself on being a prestigious place where only the wealthy and best students go. At least, that's the shit they feed everyone. I don't think for a second that being wealthy means you're the best. In fact, some of the most shady people I've met are the most wealthy and powerful."

"I believe you," I say, thinking about my aunt. "People are shady on northside, too, but not all of them, so I get that there's multiple layers to all sorts of social classes."

"I know, right? And so many people don't get that." She sticks out her fist. "Fist-bump for seeing things clearly?"

I tap my knuckles against hers while laughing. She laughs, too.

"And to answer your question about my scholarship ..." I decide to tell her because I feel like maybe I can trust her. And even if I can't, what can she do with the information? Everyone is already aware that I'm a northside scholarship student. "I don't know who gave it to me or why. Some lawyer just showed up on my doorstep about a week ago with an envelope congratulating me on my scholarship. I had to go to the city to sign papers, but again, this was all through a lawyer, and the person/people who gave it to me wanted to remain anonymous. I'm not even sure why they chose me or how they even found out about me. It was probably just random." Even when I say the words aloud, I don't fully believe them. Too much random stuff has been happening to me lately to actually be random.

"That's weird that they wanted to remain anonymous," Wren states as she absentmindedly digs a tube of lipstick out of her bag. She applies it then puts it away again before saying, "I have an uncle who's a lawyer. He helps me out with stories sometimes. I could ask him about this and see if he has any theories about it. If that's okay with you, I mean?"

"Yeah, go ahead." I fleetingly consider asking her if her uncle can look into who bailed me out of jail, as well, but that would lead to a whole other level of confession time with her, and I'm not about to do that.

Sure, she seems open-minded, but if I told her I've been arrested—twice—it could lead to judgment. Even Finn and River don't want people to know they spent Friday night behind bars.

"Cool. I'll let you know what he says." Wren zips up her bag and rises to her feet right as Lily walks out of her room.

She's rocking a short, silver dress, matching shoes, and diamond earrings. She's also sporting a pout.

"I'm starting to really hate my wardrobe," she gripes while flipping her hair off her shoulder. "I look like a beauty queen in this thing."

"Beauty queens are pretty," I tell her as I stand up.

She continues to pout. "I know, but I don't feel like I want to be beauty queen-ish tonight. I'm so sick of looking like that. The only reason I ever went with this look is because my mother made me." She slumps against the wall with her arms crossed. "I don't even know who I am. Not really. I finally have a chance to figure it out, and I just need some help because I have no idea where to start."

I feel sorry for her, enough that I offer, "I have another leather jacket you can borrow." I point over my shoulder at my room. "Fair warning, I got it from a secondhand store, and it has a tear inside, but it's perfect on the outside, and if you wore it over that dress and changed your shoes, you can go with a punk princess vibe or something?" I look at Wren like, *Are those the right words to persuade her away from this existential crisis?*

"Oh, for sure," Wren agrees, giving me a subtle nod before returning her attention to Lily. "I have these really cool black platform shoes you can borrow. And you can put on those lace tights."

With her lips smashed together, Lily pushes away from the wall. "All right. Yeah, let me try that."

"We can grab my shoes on the way?" Wren suggests then flicks a glance at me. "You want to grab that jacket, and then we can head out?"

"Sure." I hurry back to my room and collect the jacket from the closet.

As I'm heading back out, I pause as I hear Wren talking in a hushed tone.

"Are you sure you did it?" she whispers to Lily. "Because it doesn't seem like you did."

"Oh my God, Wren, for the hundredth time, yes, I did it," Lily gripes. "So, please, stop harassing me. You're starting to sound like your mother."

"I'm sorry," Wren replies. "I know this sucks, but you know what will happen if you don't ... Things would've been so much easier if we'd been roomed together in the first place."

"Shh ..." Lily hisses. "I don't want Maddy finding out."

My stomach twists. What are they talking about exactly? And why do I have this sinking suspicion it has to do with me?"

I remain inside my room for another minute to see if they'll talk more. When nothing but silence filters through the air, I give up, put on my best composed face, and exit my room with my jacket.

"Here you go." I hand it to Lily.

She smiles.

I smile back, but it's not real at all.

Finn said people here were made of plastic. He might be onto something. Because I'm already in day two, and I feel like I'm turning into a freaking doll.

Fifteen minutes later and a walk to the back of the campus, I find myself standing on a street lined with massive Victorian houses and lampposts, all of which are labeled with sorority and fraternity names. Most of the houses are quiet, but I can detect music flowing from someplace close by.

"Wow, this place is so pretty," I remark over the sound of my boots scuffing against the pavement. The air has a slight nip to it, and the branches of the trees move lazily against the night. "It's crazy it was hidden right behind those trees."

"It's so that all the dirty secrets lying behind these walls can stay hidden," Wren states as she stares at the night sky cut with silver and purple stars.

"Not this again." Lily shakes her head as she wraps the leather jacket tighter around her. She also has on Wren's platform shoes. Between the two additions, she does look punk princess. She glances at me. "Wren is really into conspiracy theories."

"They're not conspiracy theories." Wren tosses a dirty look at Lily. "They're theories based on stories I've heard from people who've lived them."

"What kind of stories?" I wonder, my attention drifting farther down the road where a handful of expensive vehicles are parked.

"I'll tell you later, when we have more time," Wren replies as she checks her phone.

I'm unsure if she will or not. After overhearing the two of them talking, I'm skeptical about the genuineness of this friendship. Not that I'm convinced they're being malicious. It could just be that they wanted to be roommates and are bummed out about it. But it felt like they were intentionally keeping a secret from me. Not that I blame them. Everyone has their secrets. Doesn't make me any less uneasy about it, though.

I might have overanalyzed this all night if I didn't become distracted by the house we come to a stop in front of. If you can even call the two-story, column-lined, massive mansion in front of us a house. If it weren't for the sign above the tall, double doors, I'd think it was a city hall.

"Okay, time for rules." Wren slips her phone into the pocket of her jacket and directs her attention to me and Lily. "We're going to stay together at all times, but if we do wander off to go hookup or something, let one of us know the where and the who." She draws this triangle pattern between the three of us in the air in front of her. "No taking any drinks or pills from anyone. If you want to drink or get high, get that shit yourself. And most importantly, do not go back to the dorms yourself. Wandering around at night, especially when we have to cut through the woods, is a dumbass idea."

Lily rolls her eyes. "Yes, Mother."

Wren points her finger at Lily. "Hey, I've heard the stories about what happens at these parties, so don't judge me."

"Maybe we shouldn't go then?" I suggest, scuffing the tip of my boot against the ground. "If it's that bad."

"Not all the parties are bad. Just a few of the partygoers. And that's generally the rule at any party." She gives me a funny look. "Not to stereotype, but they have parties on northside—I know they have to. So, why do you seem so sketched out about this?"

"Because they have parties on northside." And because of my parents. I'm not about to disclose that to her, though. "It's fine. I'm sure it'll be fine."

"Oh, it'll be something," Wren mumbles as she eyes a group of guys exiting the house.

"I'll respect your rules," Lily informs her as she runs her hands across the front of her dress, smoothing any wrinkles. "But if my brothers offer me a drink or drugs, I'm going to take it because Finn and River aren't like that."

Wren combs her fingers through her hair. "Obviously, Lils, but they're not going to offer you anything—they're too protective of you."

"Don't remind me," Lily grumbles then squares her shoulders. "Come on; let's stop standing around and being lame and go have some fun." Then she throws her fist into the air and marches forward.

Wren and I trade a wary look, and I get the vibe she's equally as unenthusiastic about being here as I am. So, why is she here?

That's an excellent question. Maybe it's just for Lily, but I feel like it might not be.

"You don't like parties, do you?" I call out as we walk up the stairway toward the entrance.

As suspected, everyone I pass gawks at me. Or, more specifically, my outfit.

I do my best to disregard it and focus on talking to Wren.

"I don't necessarily hate them!" she shouts as we step inside the house and into the foyer.

The place is packed, music is blasting from the DJ station, and furniture has been repositioned so that people can dance in the spacious living room in front of us.

"I just hate that there could always be assholes that ruin them," she adds loudly over the music as her gaze sweeps the area. She's looking for someone and spots them almost right away. "Come on. I want to introduce you to someone." With that, she snags my hand and yanks me forward in the direction of where Lily is wandering to.

We have to push past people and squeeze up against walls, but eventually, we break through the mob and to a less crowded side of the room where a game of beer pong is going on.

And on one side of the table, a blond-haired, football god, I guess friend of mine, is holding a ball and talking shit with a guy on the other side.

"Now, this"—I point at the table—"is the only thing I've seen throughout the last couple of days that is familiar to me."

She glances at me from over her shoulder. "Do you know how to play?"

I give a wicked laugh. "Dude, I'm from northside. It's like a requirement to know how to play. In fact, they won't even let you graduate high school unless you play a beer pong competition."

She snorts a laugh. "You're funny." Then she almost instantly gets distracted. "Wait, where the hell did Lily go?"

I stand on my tiptoes and peer around, looking for a halo of blonde hair. "Oh, found her." I point to the corner of the room where Lily is standing with her hand pressed against the chest of a guy with dark, chin-length hair.

Wren tracks where I'm pointing then frowns. "Oh, hell no, she did not just go after freaking James. I thought she learned her lesson the last time." She marches forward, shoving people out of the way.

One of the girls she pushes stumbles and spills her drink all over her dress. She glares at Wren then at me, as if I was somehow part of it.

"What's your problem, bitch?" she snaps as she wipes off her dress with her hand.

I open my mouth to say something that will probably result in a fight, but my words are cut off as Finn spots me and shouts out, "Hey, it's my bestie."

Great. Now everyone is staring at me like I'm a unicorn that has a horn growing out of my ass.

Finn makes his way over to me, his blue eyes shining with proof that he's either drunk or a bit high. When he reaches me, he drapes an arm around my shoulders and smiles down at me. "You made it," he says, all drunkenly smiley. He smells like mint with a splash of cologne and a hint of whiskey. His gaze scrolls over me. "You look so pretty."

How is this guy for reals?

I angle my head toward him and put my hand on my hip. "Seriously?"

"Yes, seriously," he replies in all seriousness. When I give him an unimpressed stare, he bats his eyelashes at me. "What? I'm just stating a fact."

I could ream into him for the remark, but I decide to play nice for the night. "Thanks, I guess."

His lips part in mocking shock. "Did I just get a thank you from Maddison Averly?"

"Don't get used to it," I inform him. "I've decided to play princess for the night, but I'll turn into a rotting pumpkin at midnight."

He lowers his voice and leans closer to me. "Fair warning: princesses here aren't nice." With that, he slants back and returns to his glittering cheerful self. "Wanna play?" He nods at the beer pong table then waggles his brows at me.

I glance at the table where the guys he was playing with earlier are staring at us, just like everyone else. Some of them are smirking, some are glaring, and some are looking at me like I'm trash.

I should decline Finn's offer and attempt to stay out of the spotlight, but I like the idea of handing these amateur beer-pong players their asses. Because yes, as cliché as this is going to sound, beer pong is the number one game on northside.

"Sure." I have to bite back a smile when his lips part in surprise, but he hastily collects himself and steers me toward the table.

"Hey, everyone," he introduces me. "This is Maddy."

A few people mumble, "Hey, Maddy." Others choose the silent option.

Whatever. I'm good. I'm used to it at this point.

I give a wave then slip out from underneath Finn's arm and stand in front of the table.

"Do you know how to play?" he asks me as he picks up the ball.

I nod. "Sure. I've played a few times." I stick out my hand, and he drops the ball into my palm.

Smiling to myself, I turn and bounce the ball against the table. When it lands in a cup, everyone looks shocked as hell.

"Holy crap," one of the guys across the table mumbles.

A smile breaks across Finn's face. "Why do I get the feeling that wasn't beginner's luck?"

I merely shrug, and his smile broadens as he sticks out his fist for a fist-bump.

I tap my knuckles against his, and he laughs before facing the table again.

For the next twenty minutes, we continue to play. At a certain point, Wren comes to check on me but seems okay when she notes I'm with Finn and wanders off to keep an eye on Lily. I end up having to take three drinks, and it turns out, they're not playing beer pong, but whiskey pong. I'm not a fan of that at all. My tolerance for alcohol is super low, so I'm fairly buzzed at this point.

And I have to pee.

"Where's the bathroom?" I ask Finn, leaning in so he can hear me over the music.

He has the ball in his hand but pauses. "It's upstairs." He points to a stairway behind us. "Third door on the right."

"Okay, you'll have to find another partner to play with you." I start to walk away, but he captures me by the arm.

"That's okay. I need a break, anyway." He sets the ball down on the table and backs toward a doorway behind him. "Come find me when you're done, okay?"

I give him a thumbs-up then make my way toward the stairway, squeezing past people. When I make it upstairs, I breathe in relief at how much quieter it is up here. Sure, a few people are around but way less than downstairs. And the music is more muffled.

I find the third door on the right, go into the bathroom, and lock the door. Then I slump against the door and release an uneven breath. That was a lot of socializing for me. Way too much. I'm exhausted.

I decide to text Lily after I pee and see if her and Wren are ready to bounce. Doubtful, since it's not even eleven o'clock, but here's to hoping.

My fingers feel a bit numb as I message Lily, an indicator that my alcohol level is a bit too high, and that I need to make sure not to drink anything more.

Once I send the message, I head out of the bathroom and into the hallway. Weirdly, all the people who were here a few minutes ago have cleared out. The silence and emptiness has me on edge, like when I'm wandering around in the city past dark alleyways. But I remind myself that this isn't northside, that I'm not outside, and therefore, I'm safer. But what Lily and Wren told me on the way here echoes through my mind.

"You're fine," I mumble to myself as my anxiety starts to get the best of me. "You'll be okay—"

A hand comes down over my mouth, and an arm slips around my waist. Then I'm being dragged backward toward the end of the hallway that's smothered with darkness. Panic sets in, but I work to stay in control as I lift my leg and bash my foot into the shin of the person holding me. They grunt, and it's definitely a male grunt. As their hold on me loosens, I take off, glancing over my shoulder as I do.

All I can make out is their silhouette, and that they're tall. I'm not about to go check to see who it is, though, and continue barreling forward until I reach the bottom of the stairs. The room is packed as I enter it, and my gasping for air and frantic demeanor draws a lot of attention. I cringe at how many people are staring at me and suddenly want nothing more than to get the hell out of here. I'll walk through the woods myself. I don't care.

"Maddy?" River steps out of the crowd, takes one look at me, and worry flashes across his face. He's dressed in a black shirt, dark jeans, and sneakers, and his hair is styled messily, wisps hanging in his eyes. "Are you okay?"

I start to nod then pause. "I'm ..." I cast a glance at the stairway, my brain frantically searching for an explanation as to what just occurred. "I'm not sure." I direct my attention back to him.

He wets his lips with his tongue then nods toward the foyer. "Let's go outside where it's quieter, and then you can tell me what happened."

Nodding, I remain close to him as we weave through people until we reach the front door. There, we exit out onto the front porch and into the cool night air. Then we start down the path and onto the sidewalk.

"Let's walk for a second," River mumbles with a frown as he notes that everyone nearby is staring at us.

Wrapping my arms around myself, I follow him down the sidewalk until the noises of the party are simply an afterthought. The light from the lampposts cast a soft glow across us along with the silvery moonlight.

He stops as we arrive at the corner of the street where no one is around. Then he faces me. "So, what happened?"

I recline against a lamppost. "Someone tried to grab me in the hallway upstairs right after I came out of the bathroom."

The soft glow of the lamppost reflects in his wide eyes. "What?"

"Surprised the shit out of me, too," I say. "And I'm unsure what they were planning on doing to me, but I kicked the hell out of their shin hard enough that they released me."

He rakes his fingers through his hair, his eyes roving all over me. "Are you okay? Did they hurt you?"

"Nah. They just scared me a bit. But honestly, I'm used to that kind of thing."

"Getting grabbed against your will?" he questions slowly, as if I'm crazy.

I lift a shoulder. "I worked nights at this café on the weekend, and I had to walk home since I have no car. The area was sketchy, even for northside ... so, yeah, I'm used to that sort of thing."

He silently absorbs my words. "Well, you shouldn't have to be."

"I know. But it is what it is."

He traces his finger along his bottom lip. "I'm going to try to find out who did it. I'm not positive if I can, since that isn't really my scene, but it's Finn's. So, if you're okay with it, I might get him involved."

"Sure, but it's not a huge deal if you don't find out who did it. It's not like you can really do anything to the person for simply grabbing me for a second."

He raises his brows as if to suggest otherwise.

"Or maybe not," I add at the sight of his expression.

"We'll see," is all he says before he takes a drink from his cup.

I admire his confidence, but I'm not counting on him being successful with this. I know the drill with these types of issues.

"You didn't text me," he says abruptly as he lowers his cup from his mouth.

"Huh? Oh, yeah, I got sidetracked by convincing your sister that I couldn't go to dinner with her and Wren, and then she convinced me to come to this party with her." Still leaning against the lamppost, I stretch my legs out in front of me, highly aware that the stars are a tad bit blurrier than they should be.

I shouldn't have drank tonight.

"How come you couldn't go to dinner with her?"

"I had homework to do."

"Is that the real reason?"

"Well, partly." I scratch my arm. "The other part is there's no way I could afford to go where they were eating."

"You could always have asked her to go to a cheaper place." He takes a sip of his drink. "My sister's nice, I promise. I know she probably comes off as dramatic and a bit pushy—which she is—but she'll be a good friend to you if you'll let her."

"I'm trying here." I gesture at the house where the party is taking place. "It's the reason why I'm here. Although, I spent more time with Finn than her ... She wandered off the minute we got here."

His brows elevate. "You hung out with Finn?"

I push away from the lamppost and straighten. "Yep. We played beer pong. Or, well, whiskey pong."

His eyes search mine. "You've been drinking?"

"Just a little bit." When he frowns, I tap his cup with my finger. "Dude, don't be judge-y with me."

"This is water," he explains then shows me the inside of the cup.

"It could be vodka. Or everclear."

"Smell it."

I do. It's water, for sure.

"I don't drink. Not during the season, anyway," he explains. "And I try not to because I'm a terrible drunk."

"Do you get angry or something?" *Like my father does.*

"No, I cry, actually," he confesses with a drop of embarrassment.

His confession throws me off so much that it takes me a flicker of starlight to speak again.

"You know, you don't match my first impression of you," I finally say. "Unless this isn't the real you."

He stares down at his cup. "It is, and it isn't."

My head angles to the side. "What does that mean?"

He quietly exhales then lifts his gaze to mine. "It means I live a life where I have to have different versions of myself."

The breeze picks up, blowing strands of hair into my face. "That sounds kind of depressing."

"Why do you think I cry when I get drunk?" he quips. Then he drags his fingers through his hair and abruptly changes the subject. "So, about training you ... I was thinking that we could meet in the mornings and run. I usually run with a group of guys, but we also run in the evenings, too, so I can just do that with them then."

"You want to run with me?" I double-check, surprised.

"If that's okay?" he answers. "I mean, it's the best way to train you."

"Yeah, if I can keep up with you." Not that I think I'm slow. I'm just being a realistic.

"We can go at your pace. And then I'll have my evenings for my training." He briefly hesitates. "Unless you don't want to."

"No, I do. I just ... Are you sure you want to? Because I thought you were just going to give me some pointers?"

He dithers. "Don't take this the wrong way, but if you want to make the team, you're going to have to improve your times a bit. Not that they're bad. They just need to get slightly better."

I study him. "How do you know what my times are?"

He squirms, avoiding eye contact with me. "I looked you up online."

Okay, as weird as this might seem, I kind of like that he did —I did the same to him.

Not that I like like him or anything like that.

"You looked my times up, huh?" I can't stop a smile from touching my lips at how squirmy he's gotten.

"I wanted to see what kind of training you needed," he stresses. "I kind of had to."

"Or you could've just asked me. Or were you too shy?" I tease, nudging his foot with mine.

He shakes his head but struggles not to smile. "Well, maybe I would have if you'd texted me."

"All right, fair enough." I'm smiling now, which is odd, considering only minutes ago, some guy tried to drag me down the hallway.

That reminder sends my mood plummeting and also reminds me that I need to check and see if Lily messaged me back.

"Your times are good," he tells me while I'm digging out my phone from my pocket. "And I'm guessing you ran them without a personal coach."

I snort a laugh. "No, no personal coaches ever. And my high school coach was the gym teacher who couldn't even run himself, so I basically trained myself."

Lily has sent me a message.

Lily: If you're ready to leave, that's totally fine with me. But can you wait like twenty minutes or so? This guy that I like so much is finally talking to me!

"What's up?" River asks.

I pocket my phone. "I'm kind of ready to leave this little shindig, but I don't think your sister is. And I don't have Wren's number." I briefly pause. "Is there like a way back to campus where I don't have to walk through the woods?"

"Are you thinking about walking back by yourself?" He doesn't seem to like this idea.

"Maybe, if I don't have to walk through the woods." I yawn. "I'm exhausted, honestly. I don't drink a lot, either, so my body's not used to this."

He rubs his lips together. "I can walk you back to your dorm."

"You don't have to do that. I've already ruined too much of your night."

"Trust me; you haven't ruined anything. Like I said, this isn't really my scene."

"Why are you here then?"

"Appearances," he says flatly. "I'm obligated to because of my last name."

I wrap my jacket tighter around myself as the wind picks up even more. "Are you in the frat?"

"Technically. But I barely associate with it unless I have to." He dazes off momentarily before blinking and returning his gaze to me. "Let me walk you back to the dorms. You really shouldn't be wandering around at night by yourself."

His words strike me hard because he's right. I probably shouldn't, and yet that's all I've done since I was four years old. It's tragically sad in a way that makes my chest ache.

"All right, gothic prince, you can walk me back to my dorm." I smile in an attempt to lighten the mood.

"Gothic prince?" he questions as we start to walk in the direction of the woods.

"What? It seems fitting." I retrieve my phone and send Lily a quick text about what's going on. "The first time I saw you, that's kind of what I thought. Although, you were dressed a bit differently then."

"That's because Finn and I weren't hanging out in Royal City, so I felt more comfortable being myself."

"I hate to break it to you, but you still looked wealthy," I say as we step onto the path that snakes through the trees.

"Really?" His disbelief is absolutely adorable.

"Yes, really." I playfully bump my shoulder into his. "That leather jacket and fancy watch outed you."

He stuffs his hands into his pockets. "I guess I didn't really think about that."

"I'm surprised you weren't robbed." I swing around a bush in the path we're heading down.

With the branches canopying above us, the moonlight has slipped away, giving the surroundings an ominous sort of vibe. I become highly aware of how dumb of an idea it was to consider walking back by myself. Crossing my fingers, too, that River is a trustworthy person.

He frowns as if this just occurred to him.

I cover my mouth to hide my impending laugh. He totally notices, though, and narrows his eyes at me.

"Are you laughing at me?" he questions. He's not angry, though. Honestly, he appears slightly amused.

"Sort of." I lower my hand as my smile breaks through. We've reached the end of the path, and I'm grateful as the dorm building comes into view, because I'm feeling a bit dizzy from the alcohol. "I'm sorry. It's just that it's cute how naïve you are about certain things."

"I'm not naïve," he argues. When I raise my brows, he sighs. "Okay, maybe I am about northside, but here, I'm not."

"Fair enough."

"And maybe you're naïve in this world."

"Maybe." I probably am, honestly. But I'm not about to give him that.

We fall into silence as we make our way down the sidewalk and toward the entrance of the building. The sprinklers are on, and the light spritz is the only sound that can be heard, except for crickets. The sidewalks that cross the academy yard are a series of crisscrosses and mazes, yet he appears to know exactly where to go, veering left then right.

"Maybe we could trade secrets," he suggests as we reach the door to the main building. He digs his phone out to scan the code to get inside. Once it buzzes open, he holds the door open for me, and we walk in. "You know, like you teach me about northside, and I'll teach you about the ins and outs of the academy."

My shoes squeak against the floor as we start down the hallway lit up with faint lighting from a few chandeliers that have been left on.

"You really want to help me with something else?" My stomach is starting to twist with the burn of lingering whiskery that I drank earlier. "On top of helping me with my running?"

He lifts his shoulders then stuffs his hands into his pockets. "I don't mind."

I question why. Why is he being so nice to me?

I'm about to ask him when we arrive at the door to my dorm room. Suddenly, he slams to a halt with his eyes locked on the door.

"What the hell?" In the low lighting of the empty hallway, he looks pale.

I track his gaze, and my stomach churns.

"*You shouldn't have come here,*" is written across my door in paint that bleeds down the surface ever so slightly.

"What the hell?" I murmur, and then it hits, vomit burning in my throat. "Shit, I think I'm going to throw up."

My eyelids flutter open, and the first thing I notice is that my head is pounding. The next thing is that my mouth tastes like ass.

"What the hell?" I groan as I move to sit up. The movement makes my stomach muscles throb. That's when the memories start trickling back to me.

The party.

Whiskey pong.

Getting grabbed.

Leaving with River.

The note on my door.

Getting sick.

Vomiting.

Wanting to die.

River ...

River holding my hair ...

River telling me that everything will be okay ...

I groan again as I recall how he witnessed me puking at least three times. While the memories are hazy, I know he took care of me, holding my hair back while I puked, then he helped me to my room.

I think I passed out after that.

Why did I drink last night?

Better yet, why is River being so nice?

I check the time and hate myself even more. I have class in an hour. How the hell I'm going to make it through it is beyond me, but I have to.

Dragging my butt, I sit up, lower my feet to the floor, and stand up. For a flash of a moment, I think I'm going to puke again, but it's a false alarm. Taking a deep breath, I collect a pair of torn jeans and a T-shirt before heading out of my room.

Lily is in the sitting area, reading a book, with her hair pulled up, and she has sweatpants on, which is kind of an odd thing to see.

When she spots me, she closes the book. "You're alive!"

"Barely," I mumble as I trudge across the room. "I feel like I may have died last night and been resurrected."

"So, you're saying you're a vampire?"

"No way. I feel more along the lines of a zombie right now."

She snorts a laugh as she rises to her feet. "I'm sorry. I feel like this is my fault for basically making you go to the party."

"You're fine. I'm the one who chose to drink."

"Still, I feel like I shouldn't have taken off at the party and left you. And with Finn. I mean, I love my brother to death, but he likes to drink and party."

"Lily, I swear it's fine. It's not Finn's fault. It's no one's fault but my own."

She doesn't appear convinced as she gathers her book and a bag that's sitting on the coffee table. "I have to leave for this yoga class Wren and I are taking, but I'll be back in like an hour. If you need anything at all, text me, okay?"

I nod, even though I won't, and she starts for the door, throwing me a wave.

When she exits, I note that the message that was written on the door last night is gone.

Did Lily get it cleaned up? Or was it River? Probably the latter since Lily didn't mention it to me. I feel like an ominous message on the door is going to be on the conversation agenda list.

I wish I'd have at least gotten a photo of it, because I feel like it needs to be looked into. Unless it wasn't for me ...

I'm pretty sure it was, though.

I'll talk to River about it when I see him again, after I apologize for him having to take care of my pathetic ass last night.

I remain in the shower for longer than I should, desperate to scrub off last night's events. I wash my hair then climb out, dry off, and get dressed. I brush my teeth way longer than required. By the time I'm finished, I feel a tad bit better and am even slightly hungry. Food will have to come later because I need to get to class.

I'm heading toward the door with my bag slung over my

shoulder—my laptop in it—when someone knocks. I tense. Getting grabbed last night and the message on my door has me on edge.

Hesitantly, I open the door.

River is standing on the other side. He's wearing a pair of baggy sweatpants, a T-shirt, along with sneakers. He also has what looks like a to-go box in his hand.

His gaze fleetingly sweeps across me. "You're alive?" he jokes.

"Barely. I told Lily I think I died and came back as a zombie."

His lips quirk. "You did basically puke your brains out last night."

Guilt and embarrassment weave through me. "I'm so sorry. I feel like an idiot."

He grows serious as he shakes his head. "You don't need to apologize. Everyone's gotten too drunk at least one time in their life."

"I know, but how many people have gotten too drunk in their life and made some guy, who barely knows them, take care of them while they yakked their guts out."

"You didn't make me," he stresses. "In fact, you told me to leave like a dozen times."

I fidget, crossing my arms. "Why didn't you, then?"

He shrugs. "Because you were sick and could barely hold your head up. I wouldn't leave someone like that—ever." He pauses, and a trace of amusement glitters in his eyes. "And while I saw things last night that will probably haunt my nightmares, I'm glad you seem semi-okay now."

I shake my head while biting back a smile. "So, you have a joking side to you? Again, you surprise me, River Averson."

His brows knit, as if he didn't realize he had been joking with me. Then he hastily clears his throat. "So, I brought you a burger. Whenever Finn gets trashed, he likes to eat burgers because he says the grease makes his stomach feel better." He hands me the to-go box.

I take it from him, looking from the box to him. "You brought me food?" I ask, flabbergasted. No one has ever done something like this for me, and my mind doesn't even know how to process it.

He nods, brushing strands of his hand out of his eyes. "You seem shocked by that?"

"I ... I'm just not used to people doing stuff like this for me." I shake the shock out of my head. "Thank you." It might be the most sincere thank you I've ever given.

"You're welcome." His gaze flicks down the hallway as a guy shouts, "River, hurry up. We're going to be late." He returns his focus to me. "I have a weight class I have to get to, but if you need anything, just text me ... Wait, we should probably exchange numbers, right?" He leaves the question hanging in the air between us.

"Yeah, probably." It's a new experience for me as I retrieve my phone and we message each other. I've never given my number to a guy before, but that's okay. I can have a guy for a friend.

That's what I tell myself as I program River into my phone under the title, *"Gothic Prince."*

"All right, I'll text you later if I haven't heard from you, so we can figure out what time to meet in the mornings for training." He begins to back away, slipping his phone into his pocket.

"Wait just a second," I hiss, causing him to pause. I motion for him to come close, and when he does, I ask, "What happened to the message on the door?"

"I had it cleaned up," he explains while peering around suspiciously at the people roaming the hallway. "If anyone else saw it, it would've led to gossip about either you or Lily." He looks back at me. "I did take a photo of it, just in case."

I lean against the doorframe. "Can you send it to me?"

He nods. "Are you sure it was for you?"

"I'm not positive," I reply. "But I do think it's weird that the same night I got grabbed at a party, a message was left on my dorm room door. Maybe it's a coincidence. I don't know. Would anyone leave a message like that for Lily?"

He wavers. "Honestly, there's a small chance it could be for her ... She's had some problems with getting bullied before." Tension flows off of him. "Please don't say anything about that to her. And if you could keep quiet about the message on the door until we can figure out more about it, I'd really appreciate it."

While I loathe the idea of keeping a secret from Lily—or anyone—I also know that I owe River. Big time.

"I can do that," I say, checking the time on a clock on the

wall across from us. "It's the least I can do for you after you spent last night watching my stomach give itself an exorcism."

He smashes his lips together, on the verge of smiling again. "You're fine, Maddy. I'll see you later, okay?" He wavers then spins on his heels and walks off down the hallway.

I watch him walk away, convincing myself that I'm not staring at him for that long.

But the truth is, I am.

The brutal truth is, I think I might like River Averson. And that makes me uncomfortable, more than even the note on the door.

SEVENTEEN
RIVER

I've felt lonely my entire life, even when I'm with my brother or with friends and family. Because I'm the firstborn.

Yeah, Finn and I are twins, but I came into this world first. So, I'm officially the heir to my family's fortune and business. I'm also obligated to marry whoever my parents want. Sure, I could deny them, but that would leave my family's fortune and business to fall apart. And that would leave my siblings with nothing. I can't do that to them, so I live this life where I have no say in anything I do.

And I feel alone.

But then I was in jail, and I saw Maddison talking on the phone with her mother, and I felt this connection, like this beautiful girl was in the same boat as I've been in my entire life. The one where I had to take on too much responsibility at a young age. The one where I feel broken but do my best to keep it together.

I've never felt that with anyone ever. And I never thought I'd feel it with a girl from northside. The problem is nothing can come out of this other than a friendship, even if I find myself staring at her long legs and beautiful eyes far longer than I should.

She's so beautiful it's insane. But I can't act on it.

My arranged marriage may not take place until I'm twenty-one, and my parents never set a rule where I can't date until then, but what would be the point? I date and what happens if I fall for someone? Then I break their heart, and mine, and I spend the rest of my life aching with the memory of what I lost.

No, things are much better this way.

"So, I heard a rumor about you." Finn appears in my line of vision as I'm lying on the bench, about to lift a set of weights.

The sound of clanking weights fills the air, along with the stench of sweat.

He has his blond hair pulled back, and he's sporting a T-shirt with the Royal Academy Ravens football team logo on it.

I grip the bar. "Isn't there always a rumor going around about me?"

He moves around and stands near my head to spot me. "Sure, but this one was more interesting than any other I've heard."

I grunt as I lift the weight. I already know where he's going with this, so I don't even bother asking before I lift.

"And it has to do with a pretty northside girl who's got more snark than anyone I've ever met." His hand follows the bar as I lift it up and down. "She plays a mean game of whiskey pong, too."

I lift one more time before setting the bar down. Then I sit up and grab my bottle of water. "You shouldn't have talked her into playing that. She ended up getting sick."

He frowns. "Really? She didn't drink that much. At least, while we were playing."

"Yeah, but she told me she doesn't usually drink a lot." I reach for a towel to wipe the sweat off my head. "And to you, a little bit to drink is a lot for most people."

He rolls his eyes. "Only you think that."

I could argue with him, but I have more important things to talk to him about. "Whatever." I swing my leg over to the side and sit on the edge of the bench. "Off the subject just a little, but last night, while Maddy was leaving the bathroom at the party, someone grabbed her."

"*What?*"

I twist the cap back on the bottle of water. "She got away and everything. I actually ran into her like a minute after it happened, and it's part of the reason why I walked her back to the dorm."

"Sure it was," he says, like it's not the reason at all.

He could be slightly right, but I won't admit that aloud.

"Anyway, do you have any idea who could've done it?"

"No. Why would I?"

"Because that's more of your scene. Plus—"

"Don't," he hisses, flicking a frantic glance around the room. "Don't bring that up here."

He's probably right, but that doesn't mean it doesn't need to be discussed.

"Fine." I stand up and collect my bag. "But later, when we get to our dorm, we're continuing this conversation."

He throws me a dirty look and a one-fingered salute before walking off.

I exit the weight room and turn right down the hallway, heading toward my dorm so I can take a shower before I have to go to class. I'm halfway there when Noah falls into step beside me.

The muscle in my jaw ticks. Noah and I used to be best friends until his mother had an affair with my father, which resulted in the divorce of my parents. Noah was aware of the affair before Finn and I were, and he never thought to tell us. It was a shit move on his part, and now I no longer trust him.

"Hey, so I heard this thing about you," he starts.

"Let me guess. You heard that I was hanging out with Maddison Averly?" I ask without glancing at him.

"That's part of it." He opens and flexes his hands at his sides. "I also heard you might not be pledging—"

I grind to a halt. "You really want to have that conversation out in the open?" I question in a low tone while giving a pressing glance around the hallway.

Finn was right to stop me from discussing this very subject when I brought it up while we were in the workout room.

"I ..." He trails off. "Sorry, it's just that your father asked me to—"

I step toward him and, in a low tone, warn, "Do not mention

my father to me—ever." I could hit him—I should. I should've a long time ago when I first learned about his betrayal.

"I ..." He starts to continue with a splash of worry on his face, but I walk off before he can finish.

I won't talk to him about my father, but that doesn't make me question the fact that my father sent him to ask me about my refusal to apply for the society. I ignored their request weeks ago, and I knew then that my father would be furious about it. He already controls my every move, though, and this was my attempt to at least try to have a drop of control over my life.

So, yeah, I expected him to come after me for not joining. What I didn't expect was for him to send Noah.

It's not like Noah is a fan of his. Never has been. So, why is he playing message bitch boy for my dad?

I'm not sure, but I'm going to find out.

Going to class with a hangover was hell, but it does help when I return to my dorm and dive into the burger and fries River gave me. I've never been so in love with a burger before.

As I'm sitting on my bed, stuffing my face with this yummy goodness, I grab my phone and text River a message.

Me: Thanks for the burger. You were right. It's making me feel better.

I also note that River has sent me the photo of the message on the door last night.

You shouldn't have come here.

It's creepy as hell that it's written in red paint that has dripped down the door like blood.

River said there's a small chance the message could be for Lily. Maybe it makes more sense that it was for her. No one except a few people has associated with me during my short time here. So, why would anyone come after me like this?

Still, an unsettling feeling sits in my stomach that the message was for me. That could just be from the hangover, though.

Maybe if I eat more burgers and fries ...

I stuff my mouth with greasy goodness as I sit with my legs crisscrossed on the bed. My laptop is open in front of me, and I'm supposed to be working on some research for an assignment, but my head is complicating the task.

Ping.

The sound of an incoming message scares the ever-loving crap out of me. Once I've got my heart rate settled down, I check the message.

Gothic Prince: You're welcome. Glad you're feeling better. Do you think you'll feel better enough to meet me out by the track at five o'clock tomorrow morning?

I cringe at the idea of getting up that early, yet he's been kind enough to help me out, so I can force my lazy ass to get out of bed to meet him.

Me: Yep, I'll be there.

Gothic Prince: Good. I'll see you then.

I set the phone down and decide to take a powernap, knowing I'll need it to work through my hangover.

Right as my eyelids lower, a door slams, and then I hear Lily growl, "I can't believe this. Why does he do this to me? Why? Why? Why?"

I consider pretending I'm not in my room—it's not like I'm an expert at dealing with problems. Hell, I can't even handle my own on most days. Lily has been nice to me, though, and guilt trickles through me, enough that I drag my butt out into the living room area.

When I walk in, Lily is pacing the length of the room, muttering incoherently under her breath.

"Are you okay?" I ask carefully.

She furiously shakes her head. "No, I'm not. And you want to know why?" Her nostrils flare as she looks at me. "Because of my dumbass brother. He's such a liar. I know it was him. I know it was." She begins pacing again, with her arms crossed, and she keeps shaking her head.

"Which brother are you talking about?" I dare ask as I make my way further into the room.

"The one who always does this shit … No, that's a lie. Finn sometimes does it, but River is always doing this. *Always*," she emphasizes.

I sink onto the armrest of a chair and watch her pace. "Can I ask what he did?"

She slips a scrunchie out of her hair, letting her hair fall down, before gathering it back up into a ponytail again. "Well, I went to my yoga class today, thinking it would be a great day. In fact, I worked hard to convince myself it would be. But then I get there and this bitch, Amy Fellingford, asked me what it felt like to have no one want me here. When I asked what the hell she was talking about, she told me that, last night, she saw that someone painted the words, *'You shouldn't have come here'* on our door. I couldn't figure out what the hell she was talking about since there was no paint on the door when I got back last night. Then I had to endure Amy's smirk as she showed me a photo she took of our door last night and, sure enough, there it was." She's bouncing with restlessness as she continues to walk.

"I know River saw it and had it cleaned up before I could see it. This is so typical of him. He always does this and, sure, I like that he's trying to take care of me, but not telling me stuff doesn't help." She slams to a halt. "It worsens things because it allows people like Amy to blindside me."

"Um ..." I start, hoping to God she doesn't blame me for what I'm about to tell her. "I was actually with River last night when he found out our door had been painted with that message. I was pretty drunk, so I didn't know he had it cleaned up until this morning. I'm sorry I didn't mention anything—I honestly didn't think about it. But I also thought—and still kind of wonder—if the message was for me. Unless this Amy girl put it there ... I mean, do you know if she did?"

Lily slumps into the chair across from mine. "I doubt she did. She's more of a spread-rumors sort of girl than someone who would take the time to vandalize. I think she just saw it there, knew it was my dorm, and used it against me, because that's what she does." Her eyes darken with rage as she curls her hands into fists. "But River shouldn't have just cleaned it off. He should've warned me."

"Probably," I don't entirely agree, but I don't disagree, either. I have no siblings, so I'm clueless how these types of things work. "But I think he was just trying to protect you. And I think he was also helping me out, too, in a way."

Her gaze lifts to mine. "I still can't believe he brought you back to the dorm last night. River isn't usually like that."

"Like how?" I wonder. "Nice? I thought you said he was."

"I did, but I also said he was selective with his niceness." She assesses me. "Did you ever ask him for tips on the track team?"

"I did. And he offered to help me train."

Her brows elevate as she absorbs this. "You really must've made an impression on him when he hit you with his car if he just offered to train you." The corners of her lips quirk into a ghost of a smile.

Well, at least she's calmed down.

"Maybe it was the impression I left in the front of his car," I joke with a shrug.

She sputters a laugh. "Did that really happen?"

I laugh with her. "Nah, I was just messing with you." I wish I could tell her the truth about how River and I first met, but River started this lie, and I think he needs to be the one to tell her the truth.

I think I might talk to him about it because I hate lying to Lily.

She dabs the tears of laughter from her eyes with her fingertips. "Thanks. I really needed that." She stretches out her legs then stands up. "Do you want to go get some ice cream from the cafeteria? It might help with your hangover."

"Sure, but how did you know I'm still hungover?"

"Because you still look like you are."

"It's that obvious, huh?"

"Yeah, but that's okay. Like half the people here look that way right now. Finn included."

I rise to my feet. "Rumor on the street says he likes to party pretty hard."

"He does." She wanders across the room and picks up a bag from off the floor. "I think it's his way of coping with the divorce and Noah's betrayal." She scoops up a wallet that's fallen from the bag and drops it inside. "And River became even more guarded and controlled than he already was."

I start to head back toward my room to grab my wallet. "What about you?"

She slips the strap of her bag over her shoulder. "What about me?"

I stop in the doorway. "How do you cope?"

She flicks a piece of lint off the front of her shirt. "I didn't have to since Noah was never really my friend."

I rotate to face her. "But your parents still got divorced."

She dithers. "I know, but they never had a great marriage, anyway."

"Mine, neither," I divulge, surprising the hell out of myself.

When I first decided to attend the academy, I made a promise to myself to not tell anyone much about my northside life.

"That sucks," she says. "Has it always been that way?"

I nod. "What about yours?"

"Yep. It makes me wonder if I've ever seen a healthy relationship in my life."

"Agreed." I hold up a finger. "Let me grab my wallet, and

then we can pick up this conversation on our way to get some ice cream."

I step into my room and grab my wallet, fully knowing I should be resting, but I feel like Lily and I could have friend potential, and it would be nice to have a friend here. Well, besides River and Finn, if that's even what we are. Truthfully, I have no idea what Finn and River want from me.

That thought fills up too much of my thoughts as Lily and I wander toward the cafeteria. It's midday, sunlight trickles through the many windows lining the hallway, and the air smells sweet, like freshly baked cake. A light chatter filters through the space as people head to and from class.

Fewer people are staring at me at this point, but a few glances are being cast my way.

"So"—an arm lands on my shoulders, and a step later, Finn squeezes between Lily and me, putting an arm on her shoulders, as well—"I heard a rumor about you." He directs his attention to me.

His eyes are bloodshot, just like mine, and dark circles reside under them. His hair is perfectly done, though, and he's sporting a nice pair of black pants and a dark blue shirt.

"I'm sure you've heard a lot of rumors about me," I quip, noting how good he smells, and then I immediately mentally kick my ass for noticing that.

"Okay, I might have, but the one I'm talking about came from my lovely, overly grumpy brother, who told me that you were hungover because of the game we played last night." He removes his arm from Lily but keeps the other around my shoulders. "And for that, I'm sorry. I guess I just assumed since you kicked ass at beer pong, you had a high drinking tolerance. I should've asked if you were okay with drinking that much."

I give a dismissive wave of my hand. "I'm fine. You didn't force me to do anything, dude. I chose to play. I just thought you guys were actually playing beer pong."

A crease forms between his brows. "We weren't?"

"No, you were playing whisky pong," I point out. "That's not the same thing. At all."

"True." He considers this as we continue to walk. "I guess I should've pointed that out before I roped you into play, huh?"

"You're fine," I stress. "I don't know what River told you, but I don't blame you."

"You don't?"

"No."

A smile breaks across his face. "Aw, you're the nicest bestie ever."

I resist an eye roll at his cheesiness.

"Um, hello to you, too," Lily finally says loudly. "Jeez, Finn, it's like I'm not even here."

He turns his head toward Lily while pulling me closer to his side. "Hello, wonderful sister. How are you today?"

"Shitty," Lily replies, slowing to a stop in front of the doors that lead to the cafeteria. "Thanks to River and his lying. And I'd appreciate it if you'd pass along that message." With that, she reels around and stomps into the cafeteria.

Finn glances back at me with a frown on his face. "What the hell was that about?"

I so do not want to get into this brother and sister drama. "I think you should ask River or Lily."

"You don't want to get in the middle?" he guesses with a hint of shock. "That's ... new."

I crinkle my nose. "Why?"

He lifts a shoulder. "That's just not how it works around here. People love sticking their noses where they don't belong." He tugs on a strand of my hair. "I think I might have picked the best best friend a guy could ask for."

I give him a bored sort of look. "Dude, we both know I'm not your best friend."

"Why would you say that?" He juts out his lip. "That's so mean."

I can't hold my laughter in as I playfully shove him back. "Oh my God, you're ridiculous."

"But cute and ridiculous." He's all cheery smiles and glittering eyes. "Come on; admit it."

I put my hand on my hip. "Admit what?"

"That you think I'm cute."

"Nah, I'm definitely not going there with you."

He points a finger at me. "That doesn't sound like you're denying it."

"I think you already know you're good looking"—I step toward the cafeteria—"so stop fishing for compliments. I'm sure you get them all the time."

He backs up in front of me. "Maybe, but I feel like you don't give those out a lot, which makes them much more valuable."

"They're not." But he's correct about the first part.

A smirk spreads across his face. Who knows what words would've come out his mouth next—I'm sure ones that were both equally parts amusing and annoying—but a guy wearing a button-down white shirt, slacks, and shiny shoes strolls up to Finn. If he weren't here at the academy, I'd guess he was an accountant.

"Hey, I've been looking for you," he tells Finn as he drags his fingers through his brown hair. "You need to come with me."

Finn's entire demeanor shifts, the muscles in his face hardening, his posture stiffening. "Why?"

"Because I said so," the guy replies with arrogance ringing in his tone. Then his gaze skates to me, and his lips curl into a smirk. "I can see why you don't want to go, though." His gaze drags up and down me as he openly checks me out. "And who is this lovely thing?"

I'm getting creep vibes from this guy so badly it makes me shiver.

"This lovely thing is Maddy," I introduce myself. "And I'm guessing you're here to do Finn's taxes."

His brows tug together. "What? No."

"Oh, sorry. My bad." I gesture at his outfit. "So, you just choose to dress this way, then? Weird."

Finn presses me with a warning look, a move that seems out of character for him.

"You'll have to ignore Mads," Finn intervenes, tossing me another pressing look. "She's new."

Accountant Guy is blasting me with a withering look. With

his narrow face and small nose, he looks very snake-like. "Well, she needs to learn her place."

My lips part to tell this guy to screw off, but Finn beats me to the punch.

"I'll make sure she learns." He totally ignores me as I glower at him. "But aren't I supposed to be going with you somewhere?"

"Yes, you are," Accountant Guy mutters, his gaze never wavering from me. "Come on." Tearing his gaze off me, he snaps his fingers at Finn as he strides toward the exit.

I gape at Finn as he begrudgingly follows him. "Are you seriously going to let him boss you around like that?"

"I have to," he whispers under his breath. "Now go find Lily and forget about this." He walks away without waiting for me to respond and leaves me standing in the middle of the cafeteria with my jaw hanging to my knees.

I remain that way for about ten seconds with the sounds of clanking plates and conversation flowing around me. I could find Lily—I should. I only came here so I could get ice cream with her. But I also want to find out where Finn is going with Accountant Guy. Sure, it might be none of my business, but the way Finn's demeanor shifted was just plain odd. Where would they even be going? Why did he let that guy boss him around?

Why do I even care?

"Why did Finn just go with Eli?" Lily materializes by my side with a bowl of strawberry ice cream in her hand.

"I don't know, but he was acting weird about it."

"That's because Eli is a real piece of shit. Like put every

cliché douchebag behavior into one person, and you'd have Eli." She stares at the door as she absentmindedly stirs her ice cream. "I don't know why he'd go with him. Not after what Eli did to me."

I glance at her. "What did he do to you?"

She stiffly shrugs. "It's a long story that I don't want to talk about in the open, but it has to do with basically ruining my life in high school." She has a miserable frown on her face that's crammed with hurt. "Why would Finn go with him?"

I'm wondering the same thing. I may not know Finn well, but he doesn't seem like the kind of guy who would betray his sister like that.

"Hmm ..." I'm getting an idea. One that I probably should be getting, but ... "Screw it. Let's go." I motion for Lily to follow me as I jog out of the cafeteria.

"Wait ... Where are you going?" she asks as she rushes after me.

When I walk out of the cafeteria, I look left and right, and spot Finn and Eli just as they're rounding the corner. "Come on. Hurry." I take off in that direction, disregarding the wide-eyed stares. It's like people have never seen a girl running down the hallway like a lunatic. They'd be in for a real shock if they went to Northside High, where it's an anomaly not to see someone acting like a psycho.

"Maddy," Lily calls out breathlessly. "What the heck are we doing?"

I skid to a stop as I reach the corner I saw Finn and Eli disappear around. "We're finding out why your brother is doing with the prince of douchebaggery." I slowly peer around the corner.

"We look like crazy people," she whispers as she stands behind me.

"In northside, we'd look like normal people," I whisper back as I scan the hallway.

I spot a halo of blond hair that belongs to Finn right before he veers into a room.

I hurry toward the room with Lily trailing at my heels. She doesn't even bother asking me questions anymore, which is the first step of acceptance that we are officially spying on her brother.

The doorway Finn walked through is the arched entrance to the Royal Academy library, so says an engraved sign carved into the pillar above the archway. The place is quiet, but that's not surprising—it's a library after all.

The librarian, who's perched behind the counter, is around forty or so with chin-length black hair. She scrutinizes me as I rush by her.

"Can I help you?" she calls after me.

"Don't worry, Miss Mapltefied," Lily tells her. "She attends the school."

Ignoring the exchange, I powerwalk to the center of the room where a cluster of long, wooden tables are located. The ceiling is high-arched and layered with crisscrossing beams, the lights are woven with metal and glittery crystals, and encircling the entire room are towering bookshelves.

"Wow," I breathe out as I take the area in. "This is seriously like straight out of *Beauty and the Beast* or something. This place is crazy."

"You run way too fast for me," Lily sputters as she shuffles up to me. She's out of breath, and her face is red.

"Sorry," I apologize as I scan the tables for Finn.

"Don't be sorry. I'm the one who's out of shape." She's still holding her bowl of ice cream, and it's starting to melt.

"Do you see him anywhere?" I ask. "Finn, I mean?"

Lily's gaze sweeps across the room. "No. Are you sure he came in here? Hanging out in the library isn't really Finn's thing."

"No, he for sure came in here." I start toward the row of books and begin peering down each aisle, looking for Finn and Eli.

Lily trudges after me, grimacing at her melted ice cream. When I reach the final aisle and still don't spot Finn, confusion webs through me.

"I know he came in here," I mumble while scratching my head.

"It's okay if we don't find him. The next time I see him, I can just ask him why he's hanging out with Eli. Not that he'll for sure tell me the truth, but I can attempt to get it out of him." Lily stuffs a spoonful of melted ice cream into her mouth then pulls face. "And I'm done with that."

I'm half-listening to her. This makes no sense unless another exit exists somewhere.

"Hold on," I murmur as I wander off toward the back of the

room. I look around, searching for another door, but nope. Nothing.

"You're really stuck on this, aren't you?" Lily remarks as she steps up beside me.

"Not stuck. I just … I don't get where they went."

"Maybe you miscalculated the room they went into. Or maybe you didn't see them, but someone else."

"Maybe." I don't believe it, though. I know what I saw.

The only other alternative I can think of is that the library has a secret room.

My overactive imagination starts conjuring up all sorts of ideas, the biggest one being that if I pulled on the right book, one of the shelves would move and reveal a hidden room. But that's crazy, right?

I don't know because this world, this life, this building is all foreign to me.

After Lily and I leave the library, Lily has to head to a class, leaving me alone in the dorm. I should take a nap—that was my main goal today—but I can't get over how Finn seemingly vanished into thin air.

As my curiosity gets the best of me, I dig my laptop out of my bag, get situated on my bed, and start searching around online about the history of Royal Academy, particularly the building itself. But I can't access the website the info is on due to the fact that it's password encrypted.

I'm in no way, shape, or form a computer expert, so hacking into it isn't happening.

As I'm attempting to figure out a solution to this, an article in the search engine snags my attention.

HAZING RITUALS? *Secret Societies? Cover-Ups? Learn the Dark Side of The Royal Academy, a School Known for Its High Academics Also has the Highest Injury and Disappearance Rate Among Its Students.*

"WHAT THE ACTUAL HELL?" I click on the article and read through it.

It basically talks about how the academy is dusting stuff under the rug due to the fact that the students who attend the academy are from wealthy families. What really snags my attention is that the reporter who wrote the article interviewed someone who wanted to remain anonymous. And they were quoted talking about how a secret society hazed them, and it started with someone writing a message on their door. They don't quote what the message said, but reading this sends a chill through me.

Perhaps if I can get a hold of the reporter, I can persuade them to tell me what the message was—if they know, anyway. But the reporter who wrote the article is labeled as anonymous, too. However, the online journal that published it is listed there —*The Golden Crown Royalty News.*

"I wonder if Wren knows anyone who works there." Do I feel comfortable enough to ask her?

I'm not sure.

And I'm not even positive the message on my door was for me. It could've been for Lily. Either way, I want to know the truth. Because if I've learned anything from northside, it's that the more facts you know, the safer you are.

I lie down on my bed and hug my pillow against my chest. When I decided to accept my scholarship to the academy, I thought I'd be safe here. But I don't know now. And that makes me question if I'll ever feel safe.

NINETEEN
MADDISON

Somewhere between researching the school and attempting to return to doing my schoolwork, I fall asleep and stay that way the entire night. I'm woken up by the alarm I set on my phone screeching like a banshee on crack.

I blink my eyes open and, with a groan, fumble around on the nightstand until my fingers brush my phone. Then I crack my eyes open and silence the alarm. I almost fall back asleep but force myself to sit up. I rub my eyes with the heels of my hands before throwing the covers off of me.

It's complicated to get up, slip on a pair of running shorts, a tank top, and my sneakers, but I manage. I pull on a pair of sweats over my shorts, put on my sneakers, pull up my hair into a high ponytail, grab a hoodie, and endeavor into the living room with an empty water bottle.

It's dark in the room, so I flip on a lamp and pad softly over to the sink, not wanting to wake Lily up. Once my water bottle is full, I toss it and my phone into a bag and head out of the room.

The hallway is eerily silent, and through the windows, the sky is lingering with hints of nighttime, only a pale trickle of sunlight is visible as it creeps over the hill line.

"God, River, you're nuts," I mumble to myself as I make a turn toward the exit doors—

And I crash into someone with so much force I stumble back.

"Shit," the person curses. "Are you okay?"

When I lift my gaze, I discover the person I ran into is none other than Finn. He's wearing a green T-shirt and gym shorts, along with sneakers, and his eyes look less bloodshot today.

"Yeah, I'm just peachy." I adjust the handle of my bag. "Sorry about that. I'm not used to functioning this early in the morning, so I'm basically running in zombie mode."

He laughs. "Well, at least you're still amusing in zombie mode."

"Am I?" I question with an arch of my brow.

He grins, but that morphs into confusion. "Why are you awake so early?"

"Why are you?"

"I'm heading to football practice. I was just heading back to my room because I forgot my water bottle."

"Well, I'm heading to practice, too, but for running."

"Really? I didn't know that happened this early."

"It doesn't. I'm just doing a run with your brother."

"River?" He gapes at me. "Seriously?"

"Yeah, seriously. I don't know why you're so surprised by this. I think it's been made pretty known around this school that him and I are spending time today." I make a mocking gasp. "Which is scandalous, at least with the way everyone is acting."

"It sort of is," he reminds me. "Remember, my brother is betrothed."

"So? We're not dating. Hell, we're not even friends."

"You sure about that?"

"Yeah. We barely know each other."

"So? You can become friends with someone you barely know."

I fold my arms across my chest. "Oh yeah? Then what does that make *us*?"

His lips spread into a grin. "I already told you that you and I are besties."

"Okay then, bestie, I have a question for you. And since you're my friend, you have to answer."

His eyes glint with amusement. "Do I?"

"Yep." I tuck a strand of hair behind my ear. "Why were you with Eli yesterday? Because Lily told me that he used to bully her."

His expression drops. "He was just getting some notes from me."

"Let me guess, you did the exchange in the library?"

"How did ...? Wait—did you follow me yesterday?"

I shrug. "Lily was hurt that you were hanging out with Eli, and I thought perhaps it was a friendly visit between the two of you, so yeah, I followed you into the library where you disappeared."

His face pales, and the increasing sunlight trickling through the window reflects across his face and highlights his worry. "Maddy, you have to forget about what you saw yesterday." He nervously glances left then right before inching toward me.

I angle my head up to meet his gaze. "But I don't know what I saw. That's the point."

He leans in closer, his voice lowering. "And that's how it needs to stay. Trust me."

"Trust you? I don't even know you."

"Yeah, but ..." He shakes his head. "Why does this even matter to you?"

"I'm not sure," I reply honestly. "It just seems like between the message written on mine and Lily's door, me getting grabbed at the party, and now you are vanishing into thin air in the library ... this place seems kind of sketchy, which is saying a lot considering I'm from northside. And if I've learned anything from living there, it's that the more information you have, the safer you are."

"That's not how it works here," he whispers, touching my arm. "The less you know, the better."

"So, I'm just supposed to what?" I question. "Wait around until whoever grabbed me or left the message comes after me? And what about your sister? The message could've been for her."

"I ..." He trails off, his throat muscles bobbing as he swallows hard. "Can you just drop this? *Please?*"

The begging catch in his voice causes something inside me to break a little.

"Please, Mommy, I'm so hungry."

"Please, Mommy, I'm scared."

"Please, Mommy, help me."

"Fine, I'll drop it." I pause then add, "For now. But if anything else weird happens, I will start digging around until my fingers have blisters."

"Is that a metaphor?"

"Nah, I plan on having to dig up a body or two. I mean, doesn't every mystery lead to that?"

He gives me a hardy-har look but visibly relaxes. "Thank you." He offers me a smidgeon of a smile. "I have to go get my water bottle. Be careful, okay?"

I give him a salute, and then we part ways with him heading toward the dorms and me pushing out the door and stepping into the cool morning air.

The track is located on the far-left corner, beside the football stadium. The separation of the two shows how wealthy this school is whereas, at the community college, the two are combined with the field being located in the center of the track.

The air has a slight chill to it as I walk, even with the hoodie I slipped on, and the atmosphere is still, calm, peaceful. In my dreams, when I envision my future, I picture myself living in this kind of existence—

"No, just give me a second," someone says as I round the corner of the building and step onto the path that leads to the track.

A series of benches lining a sidewalk comes into my view, and standing beside those benches are four guys, one of which is Noah. He has a hood drawn over his head, but his bright green eyes are a dead giveaway that it's him.

A tall guy with auburn gets up in his face. "No more seconds. I want it now."

A shorter guy with long black hair positions himself on the left side of Noah while the third guy—a bodybuilder of a dude with cropped blond hair and sporting a tank top—moves to the right side of him. He's surrounded, and panic flashes in Noah's eyes as he steps back, bumping into a bench.

"I don't have it right now." Tension ripples through his body. "But give me until the end of the day—"

The tall guy slams his hands against Noah's chest and shoves him. Noah staggers backward, tumbling over the bench and landing on his ass.

"Time's up, Noah." Tall Guy steps onto the bench while the other two guys move around.

A fight is brewing, and shit is about to get ugly. I could walk away—I've seen a ton of fights go down, so it's not like this is new to me. Normally, I stay out of it because I don't want to get my ass kicked, too—or arrested. But they've got him outnumbered three to one. Plus, he's Lily, Finn, and River's stepbrother. While they may hate him, I would like to believe that they wouldn't want him getting his ass beat.

Sucking in a breath, I stride over to them like I'm sort of a boss bitch, which I am not, but these guys don't know me.

"Hey, there you are." I wind around the guys and straight

up to Noah, who's scrambling to stand up. "I've been looking for you everywhere."

Noah blinks up at me, puzzlement etched across his features.

"Sorry, I thought we were meeting out front." I offer him my hand, and his confusion remains as he places his hand in mine and lets me help him to his feet.

"Who the hell are you?" the guy with auburn hair asks me.

I face him, putting on my best I-give-zero-hells expression. "I'm Maddy. Who the hell are you?"

"I'm the guy who's about to kick your boyfriend's ass," he replies with a cocky grin.

"Really?" I ask, all blasé. And I can tell my inference is throwing him off. "Why?"

"That's none of your business, northside trash. And if you knew what was good for you, you'd walk away from this." He crosses his arms, his smirk magnifying.

So, apparently, he didn't know my name but knew who I was. And has given me a nickname.

Awesome.

"Hey," Noah starts, moving forward protectively.

"I got this," I cut him off with a look. Then I cross my arms and mirror the auburn guy's snotty attitude. "Northside trash, huh? So, you do know who I am. Or, at least, where I come from." I step forward, getting in his face. "But I'm guessing you have no clue how northside works, so I will lay it down for you. Your gangly, little bitch boy ass would get beat down by the most pathetic of the north-siders, which FYI, isn't me. I lay more in the middle, mostly because I have a mean right hook, like to carry a can of pepper spray and a Taser on me at all times, and I've been known to kick the hell out of guys' balls when I get really pissed off. In fact, I kicked one guy so hard he had to have surgery, and now he's impotent."

His eyes darken. "You're so full of shit."

"Wanna test out that theory?" I challenge. "Because you're standing in kicking range right now." I move to lift my leg up.

He stumbles back so swiftly he bumps into one of his friends.

I bite back a laugh, and Noah covers his mouth with his hand.

Auburn hair dude turns livid but doesn't step toward me again.

"I'm giving you an extra twenty-four hours." He points at Noah. "If you don't pay up, even your girlfriend won't be able to bail you out." With that, he reels around and storms off with his lackeys hauling after him.

Great. I have a plummeting feeling in my gut that a rumor will be whirling around school that Noah and I are dating.

"You didn't have to do that," Noah mutters once the guys are out of sight.

"I think you meant to say *you're welcome*." I bend down to scoop up a phone that's lying on the ground. "Is this yours?"

He takes it from me and shoves it into his pocket. "It must've fallen out when I tripped over the bench." His chest rises and falls as he huffs out a breath. "I'm so screwed." He reaches up, drags the hood of his head, and yanks his fingers through his hair.

"Why?" I wonder, shifting my weight.

"Don't worry about it." He starts to walk away.

I snag a hold of the sleeve of his jacket. "You owe me an explanation because I have a feeling that what I just did is going to come back to bite me in the ass."

His eyes search mine, and then he sighs. "I was supposed to sell them something, but I couldn't get the merchandise."

"What? Like steroids?"

"No," he responds too quickly. When I lift a brow, he anxiously scratches the back of his neck. "It's not steroids, but another type of performance drug ... How did you even know it was about that?"

"Lucky guess," I reply. "But mostly, it was because the auburn hair guy looked like a wannabe athlete."

"That auburn-haired guy's name is Daniel, and he may look like a wannabe athlete, but Greyson—the big dude—is on the boxing team, so Daniel could've had mine or your ass kicked. I think he just backed off because you're a girl." He pulls an apologetic face. "Sorry, that probably sounded sexist. I just meant that most guys don't feel comfortable hitting girls."

"You're fine," I assure him. "And maybe most guys around here don't, but on northside, they do." My mind drifts back to the night I was arrested when Drew and his friends jumped me. God knows what would've happened to me if the police hadn't shown up. Then again, I was arrested, so ...

"How come you came up short?" I wonder. "I mean, with

the steroids? And why are you even dealing, anyway? Because I'm guessing you don't need the money."

He wavers, fidgeting uncomfortably, heavy reluctance flowing from him.

"You owe me," I remind him again. "So, come on; tell me your story, bro."

His gaze slides to mine, and his eyes are sparkling with shocked surprise. "You're extremely pushy."

"And you're being extremely cagey. Which, whatever, I really don't care. But like I said, I just put myself on the line for you, and I'd like to know why."

He blows out a breath, his lips parting, "When I was in high school—"

"Maddy?" River's voice cuts through the moment as he walks toward us from the direction of where I was heading before I decided to intervene with this guy's drama.

He's wearing a pair of dark blue running shorts, a blank top, and running sneakers. His dark eyes shift from me to Noah, and he literally stops in his tracks. He blinks a few times then continues toward me.

"What're you doing?" He directs his question to Noah.

"Standing here, talking to Maddison," Noah replies in an even tone.

"No, I mean, why are you even out here?" Noah stops just short of him. "You don't usually get up this early."

"There's a first for everything," Noah tells him while pulling his hood back over his head. "Chill, I was just out for a walk.

And now I'm going to go get ready for class." With that, he walks away, his gaze sneaking in my direction.

I give a look that warns him this conversation isn't over.

"What was that about?" River asks when Noah is out of earshot. "I can tell Noah was lying through his teeth."

"Maybe you should talk to him about it," I suggest. "I don't want to get caught in the middle of this."

He wavers, rubbing his lips together as he studies me. "Just be careful around him, okay? He always comes off nice initially, but there's more to Noah than what he shows people."

"All right." I'm surprised he's letting this go so easily. "Sorry I'm late for our practice session. I was on time, I promise. But I got distracted with … well, you know."

"You're fine," he assures me as we walk up the path toward the track. "I always add ten minutes onto any time I give someone to meet me. I do it mostly out of habit because Finn is always late."

I smile at that. "I saw him in the hallway, running late because he forgot his water bottle."

"He's good at forgetting stuff, too." He smiles as we reach an iron gate. "And is slow to respond to text messages."

"What's he good at then?" I wonder as he grabs the gate handle and pulls it open.

"Flirting, football, pretending he doesn't give a shit when he really does." He walks through and lets the gate swing shut behind him. "He's a good guy, though. A bit flakey, but he can be a good friend if you don't mind dealing with that."

"I can be flakey sometimes, too. But that's mostly because

I'm not used to having obligations. Well, except for track and school. Those are choices, though."

"Your parents don't give you any rules?" He treads cautiously as we stop on a grassy section beside the track. Beside one of the few benches nearby is a green bag and a jacket lying on the ground.

"My mother had one rule for me, and that was not to be seen or heard. If I obeyed that, everything was peachy." I set my bag down beside his. "Of course, when I got older, she changed the rules and wanted me to be seen and heard while I was talking to her. You got a glimpse of that while I was in jail."

He rubs his hand. "What about your dad?"

My heart rate increases at the mention of my father, because not only is he a terrible man, but he's the root of most of the problems weeding my life right now.

"You know, you don't need to talk about him if you don't want to," River says, as if reading my emotions.

"Thanks." I shake off the anxiety creeping up on me and plaster on a cheery smile. "So, what exactly are we doing on this fine, sunny morning?" I peer up at the sky and note dark clouds looming in the distance. "Or I guess I should say a partly sunny morning that has the potential to get all stormy."

"Don't tell me the girl who handed Finn his ass while we were all in jail is afraid of running in a little bit of rain," River teases me with a grin.

Holy hell, this is the first time I've seen his teasing grin, and it is absolutely gorgeous. I manage to keep a level head, though.

"I did hand him his ass, didn't I?"

Laughter slips from his lips. "You really did." He walks over to the green bag and opens it up. "I'm pretty sure no girl has ever smarted off to him like you did." He takes out a bottle of water. "You should have heard him on the way home. He was rambling about it the entire way." He tips his head back and takes a long swig before dropping the bottle back into the bag.

"Well, then I guess that night wasn't an entire loss because that makes me kind of happy inside." I waver. "Although, weirdly, even though my mother blew off bailing me out, someone else did. So, I guess that's a positive, too. Being in jail definitely wasn't." An idea occurs to me, one that's a long shot, but it's worth trying. "When you guys got bailed out, you didn't by chance see or hear some rando there mentioning my name and giving the cashier lady some money for my bail, did you?"

He shakes his head. "Why?"

"Because the person who bailed me out wanted to remain anonymous, which is not only driving me crazy, but it's so weird. Nothing good like that ever happens to me." I hold up a finger. "Again, I'm not referring to being in jail as a good thing, but someone bailing me out with no strings attached is definitely not something that ever happens to me. And I've been in jail a couple of times."

"Really? For what?" he asks curiously as he grabs the neck of his tank top and pulls it off.

I try not to stare at the lean muscles carving his arms, but wow ... just wow.

I tear my gaze off of him. "Fights, mostly. They weren't

started by me." I slip my fingers into the hem of my sweatpants and pull them down. Then I shuck off my hoodie

This is the first time I've worn clothes that put my tattoos on display, and his eyes rove all over me as he takes in the ink curling up my upper thigh, a series of intricate lines and shadings that form a wolf with a moon and tear drop. I also have another one on my shoulder of a raven with purple-tinted feathers and flowers trimming it.

"So, are we going to work out, or are you just going to stand there and gawk at me?" I tease.

He blinks at me, his cheeks flushing. And holy hell, I never thought a blushing guy could be hot, but on River, the look is.

"Sorry." He gives a slight shake of his head, as if attempting to shake whatever thoughts he was having out of his mind. "I'm just not used to seeing tattoos on ... well, anyone really."

"Rich people don't get tats?" I question with a cock of my head.

"Not really," he replies. When I continue to stare at him, confuddled, he tacks on, "Many of our parents view tattoos as like a gateway drug to becoming troublemakers that will tarnish their family's name."

I snort a laugh. "That's the stupidest thing I've ever heard."

"Agreed." He leans over to stretch, and while he's not paying attention, I check out the lean muscles that line his back. The moment he straightens, I divert my gaze to the ground and hurry and go into a stretching pose.

Seriously, can I be any more obvious?

Facepalm.

River doesn't remark on what happened, so perhaps he didn't see me.

We spend the next ten minutes stretching and lightly chatting. Once we're good and stretched, River takes another sip of his water then asks, "You ready to do this?" He's on the brink of actually appearing happy.

"Yep." I adjust my hair into a ponytail. "What should we do with our stuff?"

"Just leave it here."

"Won't it get stolen?"

He shakes his head. "Even if someone wanted to steal something here, there are cameras all over the place."

"Right." And why would anyone steal anything when everyone who attends here has everything they could need?

He nods his head as he exits through the gated area. "Come on. I promise your stuff will be safe."

"Yeah, I get that now." I follow him. "On northside, our stuff would be gone the moment we walked out of here. And even if there was a camera nearby, it would more than likely be busted."

We start to jog down a path that stretches across the campus yard.

"I've only been in that area a few times, but I kind of got that vibe from it," he explains. "Someone once stole the tires off of Finn's car while it was parked in this parking garage down on the farthest side of that area."

"He's lucky they didn't steal the car."

"It has an excellent alarm system."

"A lot of people know how to disable those. The thief must have been an amateur." We reach the end of the sidewalk and head toward the path that leads off campus. "What was he doing down there?"

He presses his lips together and stares out at the parking lot area. "I can't tell you."

"Dude, you're so sketchy," I say, mostly joking. "You keep mentioning you've been in northside—and I know you've been arrested there—and yet you won't tell me why."

He tosses me a look. "You won't tell me why you were in jail."

"Hmm ..." I debate whether or not to tell him. I could, then perhaps he'll tell me. "If I tell you, will you tell me why you were?"

He considers what I said, his interest piqued. "Only if you promise not to ask questions."

I deliberate. "The same has to go for you, too."

He sticks out his hand. "Deal."

We shake on it, and I fight back a laugh. But I'm sure we look funny, running down the road, shaking hands.

"I got jumped by this group of people and was fighting back," I tell him, swatting a bug away from my face.

"You got arrested for that?"

"Yep. It's pretty ridiculous and isn't the first time something like that has happened."

He appears taken aback, his face creased. "That's the stupidest thing I've ever heard."

"But it's not the stupidest thing that's happened there. Trust me."

His eyes are wide as he absorbs this in.

"Now you go," I say as we round the corner and head downhill.

He hesitates. "We were down there for a car race."

My brows rise. "What? Like an illegal one."

He bobs his head up and down. "Yeah, and it got busted."

I want to ask so many more questions, but I promised I wouldn't.

"This no-questions thing might have been a dumb idea," I state with a smile.

He smiles back. "A deal's a deal."

"Oh, fine." I resist a sigh. "Where are we even running to? And what's the plan? Or are we just jogging for today?"

"I want to go far today and run a bit slower," he tells me as the clouds grow thicker. "Just to see where your endurance is. Then, when we get back to the track, we'll do some strides."

"My endurance is fabulous, so be prepared to be impressed." I dazzle him with a cheeky grin.

He sinks his teeth into his bottom lip. "All right, Maddison, impress me."

He quickens his pace, and I accelerate with him, both of us taking off down the hill. We continue to run for miles, all the way to where the road meets the city's border.

Traffic starts to thicken, and lavish houses and towering, sparkling buildings line the street. Each step makes more adrenaline rush through my body, and I hit this zone where my mind is in tune with nothing else but pushing forward—harder. I feel great. Better than I have in a long time.

Eventually, River slows to a stop near a café located on the corner street of a series of old but nicely remodeled buildings. People are roaming around on the sidewalks, shopping or heading to work—it's hard to tell.

He places his hands on his hips as he works to calm down his breathing. "How are you feeling?"

I put my hands on the back of my head to avoid hunching over. "Fantastic." I'm a bit breathless, and my legs have a dull ache in them, but I still feel like I could run for miles.

"Good." He glances at his watch. "That was about three point five miles. Do you think you can make it back? Your records online showed you can handle long distances, but I'm not sure where you're at right now. I know with me, my endurance varies depending on where I'm at with my training."

"I can make it back. Honestly, it'll be good for me, because I'm going to have to run to that bus stop at the end of Royal Road every weekend."

Thunder booms in the distance, causing my gaze to lift to the sky.

"Wait—what?" he asks, drawing my attention to him.

"I have to go to work. I work at this café located on the farthest edge of northside. Although, I've been looking for a new job, one that's closer to the academy, but I haven't had any luck."

"What job do you do there?" he asks as he reclines against the side of the café.

It starts to rain then, but just a light drizzle.

"I'm a waitress." I wipe a raindrop off my head. "It's not really a bad job, but like I said, it's far. Plus, there's some other complications that have come up that makes it kind of necessary for me to look for other employment."

His brows knit. "Like what?"

I shake my head as I press my hands against the side of the building and stretch one of my legs back. "That is a question related to why I was in jail, and we promised not to ask questions about that." I can feel his eyes on me, but I don't look at him.

Yeah, River is nice and everything, but I'm not about to give him all the shitty details about my life in northside.

"I think I can help you get a job close to the academy," he tells me. "It might take a few days, but let me look into a few things."

I laugh, thinking he's joking. When I glance at him, though, I realize he's absolutely serious.

My laughter fades into perplexity. "How would you do that? My resume literally consists of employment as a waitress on northside, so—and please don't take this the wrong way—but I feel like any connections you have are to companies and people who wouldn't want to hire someone like me."

"What do you mean, someone like you?" He rotates so he's facing me with his shoulder propped against the side of the building. "You're attending the academy on a scholarship, you graduated with a four-point-oh, and you broke a ton of track and cross country records at your school. That's pretty impressive."

His words make me feel uncomfortable, like my stomach is trying to fly away to the drizzling sky. I don't like it because it could lead to other dangerous feelings, like *liking* him. And I can't go there, no matter how pretty his eyes are or how he's looking at me like he one hundred percent genuinely means his words.

Honestly, this is the first nice thing anyone has ever said to me without strings attached.

"I've also been arrested," I remind him as I switch legs.

"Yeah, but nothing's on your record, right?"

"Not yet. But depending on how things go with the charges filed against me from last week, that could change."

"Maybe they'll be dropped."

"Maybe." It's hard to say for sure.

"Regardless, let me look into a few things, okay?" He wipes rain from his face, chest, and arms with his hand, and it takes all of my energy not to gawk as his fingers trail across his body.

"If you want to, I won't stop you. But it's probably a waste of time." I push away from the wall and bend over to stretch when the drizzle morphs into a full-blown storm.

"Shit," River curses as the downpour cascades over us and starts flooding the ground.

The thunder and lightning picks up, the sky lighting up with streaks of electric blue and silver.

"Holy crap, that got bad quickly!" I shout over the rain and wind.

River snatches a hold of my hand and yanks me around the building. The feel of his hand in mine causes my heart to match the beat of the thunder as it slams against my ribcage with so much force I become more breathless than when we were running.

I should pull away, but instead, I latch on and run with him as he steers us out of the rain and into the entrance of the café. Our wet sneakers squeak against the polished floor, and patrons sitting at tables glance up as we barrel in, dripping wet and still holding hands.

The place has an old-school vibe with a checkerboard floor, pink walls, and a chalkboard menu, but I can tell everything is high-end quality.

"Come on; let's go see if they'll let us use their phone," River says as he tows me with him around the tables and toward the counter.

Still holding my hand.

"Um ... you have to have a shirt on to be in here," the cashier tells River as he approaches the ordering section of the café. She's in her mid-twenties, with dark hair, and her eyes are roving all over River's body, despite her words.

"Yeah, I'm so sorry about that," River replies in a charming tone I haven't heard him use before. "But my friend and I were out running when the storm came in, and we're kind of stuck here unless I can use your phone to call someone to come pick us up. Would that be okay? I promise I'll make it quick, and then we'll go stand outside and wait under the canopy." He dazzles her with a smile, and I'm surprised she doesn't melt into a puddle on the floor.

Because it's so pretty it's alarming.

He's still holding my hand as he flirts with her, so I discreetly wiggle it from his grip.

Reluctance masks the cashier's expression. "I don't know ..."

"Please." River rests both arms on the counter and actually bats his eyelashes at her. "I would really appreciate it."

Her cheeks flush as she grows flustered. "Okay, yeah, just make it quick, okay?" She backs toward the back area and picks up a cordless phone. "My name's Eve, by the way." She hands River the phone while flitting a glance in my direction and subtly measuring me up. She's trying to figure out what River and I are.

Not wanting her to think we're dating, especially since he's flirting with her so he can use the phone, I ask her, "Is it okay if I use your restroom?"

She nods, her eyes traveling over me. A pucker forms at her brows. "Sure. It's right over there." She points at a hallway to my right.

"Thanks." I start to walk away.

"Wait—do I know you?" she asks after I've taken a couple of steps.

I twist back around. "No. I'm not even from around here."

She continues to stare at me but doesn't say a word, so I walk away and go into the bathroom. I don't have to go, but I need a breather from the fancy café, the staring, and the lingering thoughts of how much I liked River holding my hand.

What the heck is wrong with me? I've never gotten so flustered over a guy holding my hand before.

Once inside the single bathroom, I lock the door and stand

in front of the mirror, staring at my reflection. My dark hair is dripping wet, my cheeks are flushed, and my top is clinging to my skin. No wonder everyone was staring at us as we ran in. Add my disheveled appearance with River's shirtlessness, and we probably look like north-siders. So, I look like myself.

I remain in front of the mirror for a few minutes before leaving the restroom. I've warmed up a bit by then, but when I return to the counter where River is waiting for me, he tells me, "Finn's coming to get us. He'll be here in about fifteen minutes, but we have to wait outside." He nods subtly at Eve, the cashier, who's now glaring at River with her arms crossed.

"Um, okay." I trail after River as he winds around the tables and exits the café.

Once outside, the cold, wet air almost instantaneously chills my bones.

"What was that about?" I ask, nodding back at the inside of the café. "She seemed fine when I left for the bathroom but looked like she wanted to murder you by the time I returned."

"I pissed her off," River confesses as we stand under the canopy doming above the entrance doors.

"I got that, but how? Because you were charming the hell out of her when I walked away."

He faces me. "She asked if she could have my number, and I said no because you were my girlfriend."

"What? Why did you do that?" I playfully shove him. "That's so not cool."

"Sorry." He barely stumbles. "I panicked."

"You could've just given her a fake number."

"I guess." He wrinkled his nose as if that just occurred to him.

"You're not used to getting hit on?" I question. "Because it seems like you're not."

He shrugs. "Almost everyone I know knows I'm betrothed."

"Oh." I lean back against the wall beside the door. "I'm sorry."

Confusion swirls in his pupils as potently as the rain rivering down the sidewalk behind him. "For what?"

I shrug while rubbing my hands up and down my arms as a shiver rolls through my body. "I don't know. For not being able to make your own choices, I guess."

His eyes search mine. "I think you might be the first person who's ever said that to me."

"Really?"

"Yeah."

"Well, I'm sorry for that, too."

We grow silent then with rain, thunder, and cars splashing through puddles echoing in the distance. Hardly anyone is walking around now, the sidewalks basically empty. The longer we stand there, the colder the temperature drops, and no matter how tightly I wrap my arm around myself, I can't warm up.

"You're freezing," River notes as he eyes how badly I'm shivering. "You should go inside. You're wearing enough clothes that she can't kick you out."

I shake my head. "I'd rather not go back in there."

"Maddy," he starts to say.

"I'm fine," I assure him. "I'd rather stand out here and freeze for a few more minutes than get gawked at."

He rakes his teeth along his bottom lip. "I have an idea. Don't freak out." He steps toward me.

I stiffen. "What are you doing?"

"I'm just getting closer to you to block some of the cold air," he informs me as he reduces the space between us.

My breath gets lodged in my throat as he stands so close to me that I can feel the heat coming off his body. How the hell he's still mildly warm is beyond me.

Slowly, as if approaching a skittish cat, he places a hand against the wall so I'm trapped between his arms. Then he looks down at me. "Is this okay?"

I nod, working to keep my breathing even.

Usually, I'm a badass in these types of situations. But I'm also usually annoyed when a guy is crowding my personal space. I've only kissed a few guys, and those were lame as hell, mainly because every time it happened, both me and the guy were drunk, and the kisses were sloppy at best.

He sucks in a gradual inhale through his nose, as if he's struggling to breathe evenly, too.

We remain that way for a few minutes, and slowly, the coldness creeps away from my body.

"Feeling any better?" River asks softly.

I nod again while biting my bottom lip.

His gaze drops to my mouth.

My heart leaps in my chest.

Shut the hell up, heart.

River starts to lean in, and then our lips touch.

He groans, his hand cuping my cheek as his tongue parts my mouth—

Honk. Honk. Honk.

We both startle. River pushes away from the wall and spins around toward the curb where a sleek red sports car with custom tires and a spoiler is parked. The passenger window rolls down, and sitting in the driver's seat is a grinning Finn.

"Did I just ruin a moment between the gothic princess and prince?" he teases with his arm resting on the steering wheel.

My heart is beating frantically in my chest. I just kissed River. Oh my god.

"Shut up," River hisses as he marches over to the car, his sneakers splashing in the puddles.

I inhale and exhale to steady my heart before pushing away from the wall and approaching the car.

Stay cool, Maddy. No need to flip out over a brief kiss with a guy. You've kissed guys before. This is no big deal.

Except River is a Royal and he's betrothed.

Ugh, I'm so dumb.

"Okay, brother," Finn replies with amusement ringing in his tone.

River is rippling with irritation as he yanks the passenger door open, flips the seat forward, and climbs into the back.

"I'm okay with sitting in the back," I tell him as rain drips over me.

Shaking his head, he readjusts the passenger seat for me. "Sit in the front. It's more comfortable."

I want to argue that he's bigger and the front has more room, but my clothes are already getting soaked from the rain again, so I dive in and hurriedly close the door.

Finn cranks up the heat then turns the wheel and steers onto the road. He's wearing the same T-shirt and shorts I saw him in earlier, and the cab sort of smells like sweat, an indicator he came here straight from football practice.

I cringe as water drips off my hair and onto his nice leather seats. "I'm sorry I'm getting your seat all wet."

"It's fine," Finn tells me like it's no big deal that the water might ruin the leather. It could very well not be a big deal to him either. I still feel bad.

"I'll wipe it up when we get back to the school." I extend my hand for my seat belt as he speeds toward the hills where the Royal Academy is located.

Finn lets out a laugh as he turns on some music. "Don't be ridiculous. I'm not going to have you clean out my car. That's what detail service is for."

Right. Why would he want me to clean out his car when he can pay someone to polish it up all nice for him?

Once again, the reality of this world smacks me across the face.

I turn my head and stare out the window, watching the rain pour down against the streets and splatter against the pavement.

"I like your ink," Finn comments after a few streams of lyrics play.

I lift a brow at him. "Do you like it because you hardly ever see ink or because you actually like it?"

"So damn feisty," he murmurs with a ghost of a smile. He thrums his fingers to the song's rhythm as his gaze skims along the lines inking my thigh. "I like it because it's nice work."

"Finn's a closet artist," River explains from the back seat. He's leaning back with his arms tucked underneath his head.

I wonder if he's thinking about how we just kissed? Or has he kissed so much that kissing is an afterthought? I don't know... Lily made it sound like he didn't kiss a lot.

"I think, in another life, he'd try to make it as a tattoo artist," River adds.

"What the hell, bro?" Finn blasts River with a half-joking glare. "Since when do you spill my secrets? That's more of my thing."

River blinks his gaze from the window. "Sorry, I zoned out and went on auto-pilot."

"I won't tell anyone." Although, it doesn't make much sense to me why this is a huge secret. "Why does it even matter, anyway? And if you want to be one, why not just be one?"

"Because of responsibilities." He pulls a face as he returns his focus to the road. "Being a tattoo artist isn't an acceptable career."

"Why? There's some out there who are super talented and make bank." From the corner of my eye, I note an older car that's been modified but still looks oddly out of place for the glitzy streets of Royal City.

"It doesn't matter if I make bank or not." Finn shifts gears as he slows to a stop for a red light, and the older car comes to a stop, too. "What matters is that society sees me as something important, like a lawyer or CEO." He sounds miserable as he speaks.

And I think I'm getting the gist. Apparently, on top of the Averson family forcing their oldest to marry the person of their choosing, they also force them into a certain career.

"Do you draw?" I wonder, rotating in the seat to face him.

The corners of his lips quirk as he slides me a glance. "If I answered yes, then I couldn't remain a closet artist, could I?"

"Well, that's no fun at all." I rest my arms on the console and look back at River. "What about you?"

"What about me?" he replies questioningly with his gaze trained on the window.

"Are you a closet anything?" I ask, causing him to give me a what-the-hell look. I open my mouth to elaborate, but River abruptly goes rigid as he straightens in the seat.

"What the hell?" he mutters under his breath.

When I peer over my shoulder, a chill glazes through my veins.

Because Drew is climbing out of the older car parked beside us. He has on a black hoodie, holey jeans, and the hood is pulled over his head. I recognize his face, though, very clearly.

He also has a knife in his hand as he strides toward Finn's car, puddles splashing under his worn boots.

"What the hell is this dumbass doing?" Finn asks as he cranks down the music.

"He's here for me." My stomach clenches as I utter the words.

Drew raps on the window. "Maddy, get out of the car. Now."

Two more guys climb out of the car, both with their hoodies drawn over their heads. I can't distinguish their faces, but they're both tall and bulky. They don't appear to be carrying a weapon, but that doesn't mean they don't have any with them.

"Shit." I loathe how my fingers tremble as I reach for the door handle to get out of the car.

"What the hell are you doing?" River reaches between the seat and the door and grabs my hand right before I pull on the door handle.

"I'm getting out." I glance at Finn, who's gaping at me. "Don't worry. They won't bother you if I get out. I promise." I rotate toward the door and slip my hand out from River's.

"Maddy, stop." Finn quickly leans over me and captures my hand before I can pull the handle again. "I'm not about to let you get out and go with a group of guys carrying a weapon."

My attention snaps to him. "If I don't get out, this will become your problem—they'll make sure of that. And trust me; you don't want that."

"Let us decide that, okay?" Finn laces our fingers together as he sits back in the seat.

"They'll follow us if you try to drive away," I stress, my stomach spinning with nausea.

Still holding my hand, Finn casts a glance at River. "You up for navigating?"

"Sure, but I'll need your phone," River replies, scooting forward in the seat.

Finn picks up his phone from a tray under the stereo and tosses it to River.

River catches it then reclines in the seat again.

"Guys," I say, moving to unfasten my seat belt. "It's better if I get out. That car looks old and everything, but it's a modified Subaru WRX, so it's a lot faster than it looks."

"I know what kind of car it is." Finn wraps his fingers around the shifter as Drew slams his palm against the window again. "But it's not faster than mine. And besides, I'm a way better driver than that dumbass." Then, smirking at Drew through the window, Finn waggles his fingers at him while revving the engine.

I recall how River told me that him and Finn were arrested for illegal car racing, so he can obviously drive. That doesn't make me any less nervous, though. I'm bursting with nerves to the point that I feel as though I've had like three cups of coffee.

"If you go back to the academy, they'll just follow and grab me, anyway," I explain. "It's better if I just get out."

"We're not going straight back to the academy." Finn continues to smirk at Drew.

In response, Drew begins banging on the window hard enough to make the glass rattle.

"You rich piece of shit," he yells, his face bright red. "Get out of the car and smirk at me like that. I dare you."

Finn rolls the passenger side window an inch. "I'll tell you what, loser. If you catch me, I'll get out and we can hash this out any way you want."

The light turns green then and Finn flips Drew the middle

finger before peeling out, the tires squealing and spinning against the wet pavement.

"Careful with your acceleration," River warns, "or you'll hydroplane."

"I know what I'm doing," Finn replies without taking his eyes off the road.

He has one hand on the shifter and the other gripping the steering wheel as he zooms down the street, weaving through cars.

In the side mirror, I can see Drew's car chasing after us in the distance.

"Take a left up on the next road," River instructs. "It'll take us away from the traffic, and then we start heading back to the parking garage."

Finn nods, his concentration locked on driving as he steers to the right to get into the farthest lane.

My heart is pounding in my chest, and my stomach is raveling with guilt. "Guys, you don't need to do this. Just drop me off on the corner, and I'll run or something." I grip the side of the seat as Finn brakes to make a sharp turn.

"Shh ..." is all Finn says, and I get an inkling that he might be enjoying this—the race part, anyway. "Which road has less traffic?" He shifts gears, and the engine growls. "Second or third?"

"Actually, go up to fourth." River's eyes are glued to phone. "Second has heavy traffic and third is under construction."

Nodding, Finn stomps down on the gas more. We pass by cars in a blur as we zoom down the road with Drew and his lackeys hot on our tails. I have no idea where we're heading or why they think they can arrive at a safe destination, but I prepare myself for the worst because that is how this will turn out. Ultimately, the car has to stop, and I'll have to face the music—that a whisper has been put out on me. So, if Drew catches us, he'll own my ass. It's bye-bye academy, bye-bye future. What I don't understand is how in the hell he discovered where I was. His crew doesn't run southside Royal City, at least from what I'm aware of. Just like hardly anyone on northside does. So, how did I get spotted?

As Finn makes another jarring turn onto another road, my thoughts drift back to the cashier working at the café. She asked if she knew me. She didn't look familiar, and even now, I'm positive I don't know her. But if she has connections to northside, she could've heard about the whisper, connected the dots, and called up Drew.

"We're almost there," River says to no one in particular. "Hopefully, the scanner works quickly."

"It should. I just cleaned off my window." Finn downshifts as a towering building comes into view just ahead.

The exterior is reflective glass that blacks out what's on the inside. Three massive metal doors line the front section, and Finn drives straight toward the middle one that has an automatic barricade in front of it.

Traffic is thinner on the road here, so Finn can drive faster without switching lanes.

His windshield wipers are on full speed. Even then, the rain is coming down so hard it's concealing the view out the window.

But occasionally, I get a good glimpse of how we're racing toward the building. Fast. Too fast.

I squeeze my eyes shut, preparing for the worst. But suddenly, the car comes to a skidding halt. When I open my eyes, we're stopped in front of the barricade, and Finn has turned off the wiper blades.

A light flickers from off one of the barricades, and then the bar begins to lift up. So does the middle door of the building.

When I look through the back window, I see Drew's car approaching us at an alarming speed.

Finn drives through the open barricade but has to stop and wait for the door to open all the way. The barricade lowers, however, leaving it impossible for Drew to get his car into this section.

Drew's car skids to a stop just outside of it, and he jumps out. But the door is open now, and Finn slams on the gas and peels forward as Drew barrels at us. I watch with my breath trapped in my chest as Drew attempts to run inside, but the door closes before he can.

Releasing a shaky exhale, I take in the surroundings. We're in a parking garage, only a much nicer one than what I'm used to seeing on northside. This one is completely closed in, the ceilings are higher, and the area is enormous and has the occasional window that reveals the view of the buildings outside.

"Are you okay?" River asks me as he scoots forward in the seat and rests his arms on the middle console. His damp, dark hair is hanging in his eyes, and he smells like rain mixed with a trace of sweat.

I nod, even though I'm unsure if I am. "I'm fine. And, while I appreciate what you guys did, it won't stop them. They'll just sit out there and wait for me to come out."

"There are other exits out of here." Finn removes his hand from the shifter for the first time since he took off at that stoplight. "And we can access the security cameras to make sure they're not lurking outside somewhere."

"Oh." I'm still attempting to process what happened, because they just helped me for no reason, with no strings attached. It makes no sense. At least to me. "Where are we exactly?"

"The Royal City Penthouse Complex," River sets Finn's phone in the tray below the stereo. "Our family has a place here, so we can hang out until ..." His head cocks to the side as he looks at me. "Who are those guys, anyway?"

I owe them an explanation, but I wish I didn't. "It's a long story, but it has to do with the night you guys saw me in jail. Or, well, I guess that's not even when this started." No, this started with the curse of being born into my family.

River's gaze dissects me. "Those were the guys that jumped you?"

I nod. "There were other people there, too, but Drew—the guy banging on the window—is like their ring leader. We used to kind of be friends when we were kids."

"That guy used to be your friend?" Finn questions skeptically as he parks the car in an open space near the far back. Even the parking spaces here are bigger and are filled with luxury cars.

"He was until a few years ago. Then he started running with this group of people who deal drugs, and he turned into an asshole. Plus, I didn't want to be associated with that kind of shit —I already have too much of that in my life." Realizing I'm rambling, I bite down on my tongue. "But yeah, anyway."

Finn studies me for a slamming heartbeat before pushing his door open. He climbs out, stretching out his long legs, and I follow suit, leaving the door open so River can hop out. He does so with a stretch, putting his arms above his head. Then he pops his neck and shoves the door shut. Finn pushes the key fob, and the car locks with a *beep* and a flash of the headlights. Then we start toward an elevator in the far-left corner.

"So, if that guy used to be your friend," Finn asks as he pockets his key fob and phone, "then how in the hell did he end up so pissed off at you that he'd try to chase you down in the middle of the city?"

We arrive at the elevator, and beside the doors is a small screen, to which Finn swipes his thumb across. The screen illuminates, revealing a code box, and Finn punches in a few numbers. The elevator doors glide open with a *ding*. And I'm left standing there with my jaw hanging to my knees.

Finn strolls into the elevator, and River takes a step forward, but when he notes my expression, he pauses.

"What's wrong?" he asks.

"It's nothing." I feel so alarmingly out of place as I step onto the elevator that has marble floor and windowed walls.

"Clearly, it's not nothing." River gets onto the elevator, too, then slants against the back window that shows a view of a pool located in the center of a landscaped park trimmed with flourishing trees, the leaves crisp with autumn.

I stand away from the windows, not wanting to touch any of the polished surfaces and leaving smudges. "I'm just not used to all this." I gesture at the windows as the elevator doors slide shut. "Everything's just so … nice."

Finn and River trade a look, and then Finn grins at me. "Relax." He drapes his arm around me and pulls me against him. "It's not a big deal, I promise."

"It is, too, a big deal," I insist. "Everything is just so nice and clean, and I feel like if I touch anything, I'm going to ruin it."

Finn rubs his free hand across his mouth to conceal a smile.

I narrow my eyes at him. "It's not funny, so stop smiling."

"I'm sorry," Finn apologizes, but his smile breaks through. "It's just that you're so damn adorable."

"I told you to stop calling me that," I warn. "And FYI, you smell really bad."

His lips part. "I do not."

"You do, too." I smile sweetly at him. "And that's payback for calling me adorable."

"So, let me get this straight," Finn says amusedly. "I call you adorable, and you return the favor by telling me I stink?"

I shrug. "I'm not adorable."

"So, I don't stink then," Finn states.

"No, you definitely stink." I exaggeratedly fan my hand in front of my nose.

River snickers from behind us.

Finn shoots him a dirty look, to which River responds with another laugh.

"Sorry, but this is hilarious," River tells him apologetically then looks at me. "He's not used to hearing the truth. Usually, everyone kisses his ass."

"Like you're one to talk," Finn quips. "Everyone kisses your ass, too."

"No, they're afraid of my ass." River crosses his arms and stares out the window as the elevator goes so high that the pool looks like a tiny puddle.

"Are they?" Finn challenges. "Or do they think you're just anti-social?"

They continue to argue, but I barely hear them as my legs wobble. This is so high—too high. And yes, I suffer from acrophobia. For a good reason, too. When I was younger, my father and his brother—my uncle—thought it would be hilarious to dangle me over the edge of a tower they used to go to near the canal to deal drugs. It was stories high, and I don't know what the purpose of it was. All I know is that one day, when I was about six, I wanted to see where they went when they took off, so I snuck after them. When they caught me, they forced me to climb up the rusty ladder that stretches to the top of the tower. Then they dangled me over the edge, upside down, to teach me a lesson about sneaking around.

I'm honestly not even sure why I followed them. I hate my uncle, and although I wasn't aware that I did back then, I despise my father.

"Maddy?" River's worried voice slices through my memories.

When I blink back to reality, Finn and River are staring at me with concern.

"Huh?" I have no idea what's going on.

"You're shaking," Finn states, and I become painfully aware that his arm is still draped around my shoulders.

I instinctively duck out from underneath it, but the move puts me closer to a window. I freeze and let out a groan as vertigo slams through me.

"Hey." River steps forward and captures my hand. "Tell us what's wrong so we can try to help?"

"I'm afraid of heights," I moan as the elevator slows to a stop. "I just need to get off this thing."

Like the gates of heaven have opened up, the elevator doors glide open at that moment.

River walks forward, pulling me with him as he exits the elevator. Finn trails after us with his hands stuffed into his pockets and his gaze straying to mine and River's interlocked fingers.

"You okay?" he asks, meeting my gaze.

"Yeah, sorry about that." I catch my breath then stand up straight. "I just didn't realize we would go up that high."

River squeezes my hand. "You don't need to be sorry for anything." He lets go of my hand then and starts forward.

Finn steps up beside me. "You, Maddison Averly, are becoming a real mystery to me."

My head tilts to the side. "Why's that?"

He lifts a shoulder. "You just are." With that, he whisks by me.

I turn to follow him when I finally acknowledge my surroundings.

"Holy effing hell," I whisper under my breath as I take in the spacious room I'm standing in. Thick gray columns line the dark walls, and the beamed ceiling is trimmed with coiled metal lights. Filling up the room is a series of leather sofas, a few tables, along with sculptures, paintings, and a fountain. The floor is as shiny as the elevators but much darker with splashes of silver.

"This is where you guys live?" I gape at everything in awe as I follow Finn and River through the door and down a wide hallway lined with shelves of books.

"Sometimes," Finn replies as he carelessly tosses his keys onto a table that's at the end of the hallway.

"*Sometimes*," I mouth. I mean, I knew they were wealthy, but this is a whole level of rich that I can't even comprehend.

I do not belong here. I should turn back, but I'm too curious now to see the rest of the place. Plus, turning back means going into the elevator.

Once we reach the end of the hallway, we make a turn and the space opens up into a living area with one wall entirely made of windows—yeah, I'm totally going to avoid going over there.

"I need to take a shower," River announces as he starts toward another hallway.

"So do I," Finn states but doesn't head in the direction of

where River is wandering. Instead, he comes to a stop and faces me, his eyes roving over me.

"What?" I ask almost defensively.

"I was just wondering if you wanted to take a shower, too. You can use the one in Lily's room." The corners of his lips curl upward. "Although, if you want to take one with me, I'd be perfectly okay with that."

"Finn, Jesus Christ," River calls out disapprovingly as he stops in the middle of the hallway. "Stop hitting on her."

Finn breezes at me. "He's just jealous because he wishes he could."

I can't help thinking about how River kissed me. Finn must've not seen the entire thing or else I feel like he'd be mocking the hell out of us. Part of me wants to glance at River to see his expression, see if he's thinking the same thoughts I am.

But I keep my gaze on Finn and make a big show of rolling my eyes. "Yeah, right. I get the feeling he has to say that to you all the time."

His grin widens. "Okay, maybe. But it usually doesn't bother him as much."

"Finn, seriously, shut the hell up," River interrupts in a sharp tone.

When I glance at him, his eyes are firing daggers at Finn.

Finn holds his hands up and steps back. "Sorry, brother." He sounds anything but sorry.

Shaking his head, he fixes his attention on me, his eyes softening a drop. "Maddy, if you'd like to take a shower, you're more than welcome to use Lily's, and I'm sure she wouldn't mind you borrowing some of her clothes."

I have no desire to use or borrow anything here, but I'm also covered in old sweat and rain, and I feel disgusting.

"Yeah, okay, that'd actually be nice." I smile at River. "Thanks."

River motions for me to follow him. "Come on; I'll show you where her room is."

I walk over to him, throwing a wave at Finn from over my shoulder.

"Don't do anything I wouldn't do," he calls out after us with a wicked laugh.

River heaves an exhausted sigh. "Just ignore him. He's in a mood."

"Weird, because I feel like he's been in that mood since I met him," I remark, causing River to chuckle under his breath.

"Yeah, he's generally like that." He yanks both his hands through his hair, leaving strands sticking up wildly in all sorts of directions. "I'd like to say you get used to it, but I still haven't, and I've known him all of my life. It's not all bad. Sometimes, when I'm in a bad mood, it comes in handy."

"I can see that," I reply as my gaze roves over the photos hanging on the wall of landscapes and portraits of places I could only dream of seeing. "You two seem so different. It's crazy you're twins."

"We used to be similar, but then ... things changed." As if matching his words, River's mood changes, tension flowing from his now calculated steps. "But, anyway." He clears his throat as he slows to a stop in front of a shut door. "This is Lily's room. She probably hasn't been in it for over a year, but a maid comes here once a week to clean the place, so everything should be good to go." He pushes open the door. "There's probably no soap in the shower, so let me go grab a bottle of mine for you." He hurries off down the hallway. And I try not to stare at his ass or the lean muscles of his back. I fail.

Why the heck did I have to let him kiss me? This guy is so off-limites.

"Get it together, Maddy," I mumble to myself as I tear my eyes off River.

Carefully, as if entering a museum, I step into Lily's bedroom. The theme of silver and blue is splashed all over the place from the walls, to the comforter that covers the massive king bed, to the curtains and the chandelier. Even the dressers and nightstands are silver, and the knobs are baby blue. I couldn't imagine having a room like this, but it would be nice. Hell, I'd settle for the closet, which is an open area in the corner with benches and mirrors lining the wall.

"Here you go," River says as he returns with two bottles. He hands them to me, and when he notices my expression, his forehead creases. "You have a weird look on your face. Are you sure you're okay? Or is it the height thing? You can keep the windows closed, and there are none in the bathroom."

"No, it's not that." I hug the bottles of soap and shampoo against my chest. "I'm just not used to being in places like this. I mean, this room is like really, really nice—this whole place is—and it feels wrong that I'm in here, if that makes sense."

He promptly shakes his head. "Don't think like that. You belong here just as much as anyone else. Trust me." Smiling, he reaches out and tucks a strand of my hair behind my ear.

The move stuns both of us, and when my eyes go huge, he jerks back, clearing his throat for the second time in five minutes.

"Um ... yeah." His cheeks tint pink, and it takes all of my strength not to smile. "So, I texted Lily, and she said you can borrow anything. Her closet is over there." He points to it then to another doorway to our left. "The bathroom is over there. There should be towels in there already. And then, when you're done, just come back out into the room at the end of the hallway. Either Finn or I will be in there."

"Thanks." I smile, and he returns it before starting to leave. But then an overwhelming sense of gratitude falls over me. "I mean that, River. Thanks for all of this. For running with me. For helping Finn in that high-speed chase so we could escape Drew."

He nods with his hand on the doorknob. "Of course." He starts to shut the door but pauses. "I don't want to pressure you into telling me what's going on with this Drew guy, but if you feel like talking, I'm good at listening and solving problems."

"I'll keep that in mind." I force a smile, and he shuts the door. Then I exhale all the tension I've been holding since Drew showed up.

A part of me wishes it could be that easy, that I could tell River everything, and he could conjure up a solution. But while he may be a great problem solver in Royal City life, northside problems are a different ballgame.

TWENTY
RIVER

I try not to think about Maddy showering at the same time that I am, but she creeps into my mind as I stand under the showerhead, letting the warm water cascade over me. Her long legs, and the way her tattoo curled around her thigh ... her big eyes ... her toned abdomen ... those full lips that I kissed while we stood out underneath that canopy ...

I have no idea what I was thinking when I did that, other than want.

Want.

Want.

So much want.

"Dammit," I curse as my thoughts become consumed by Maddy.

I've never had this problem before. Sure, I've thought other women were hot, but I've never become infatuated with someone this fast. It's that stupid connection I felt with her when our gazes locked while we were both stuck in jail ...

Well, that and her smile ...

And body ...

And the way she makes me smile ...

I groan in frustration at my brain's inability to turn off. It needs to because we can't go there. It'll be disastrous if we do—heartbreaking, really. Because nothing can ever happen between Maddy and me but a hookup, and I feel in my soul that she's just not the kind of girl I can do that with.

Too much of a connection exists already.

After spending an unnecessary amount of time in the shower, I eventually turn on the cold water to cool off, climb out, dry myself off, and then get dressed in a pair of jeans and a T-shirt before returning to the room I instructed Maddy to go to once she's finished cleaning up.

She isn't there yet, but Finn is lounging in one of the sofas, scrolling on his phone. His hair is damp, and he's changed into gray pants and a black shirt.

"She's still in the shower," he says without glancing at me.

"I didn't ask." I sink into a chair across from where he's sitting and stare out the window.

The sunlight is now peeking through the clouds and reflects against the nearby buildings, giving the city a sparkling illusion when, really, shadows and darkness lay underneath the surface.

"But you were thinking about it." He taps his screen before setting his phone down beside him. Then he tucks his hand beneath his head and looks at me. "You were probably thinking about her while you were taking a shower, with how long it took you."

I pick up a throw pillow and chuck it at him. "Shut the hell up."

The pillow smacks him in the face, but he merely laughs. "That didn't sound like a denial."

I bounce my knee up and down, restlessly anxious at the subject, so I change it. "Why do you think that Drew guy was so determined to get a hold of her?"

Finn lowers his feet to the floor as he sits up. "I don't know. I wish she'd just tell us so we could help."

"You don't know if we can when you have no clue what the problem is."

"Every problem has a solution." Finn gives me a look. It's the same look he has been giving me since our father informed me that I'd be marrying Isla. Finn believes a solution exists, but he also dodges around many of his responsibilities without having to deal with consequences, leaving his outlook on life slightly different from mine.

"Still, just letting Father win, then, I see." He folds his arms and the muscle in his jaw ticks. "I wish you'd fight back."

"It's pointless." What I don't say is that if I did, and somehow managed to get out of the arrangement, it'd probably fall onto Finn. And he's not equipped to handle that.

"Whatever." Finn slants forward, rests his arms on his knees, and twists the ring on his finger. "While we're discussing problems, I think I should bring up one that I'm aware has to do with Maddy."

I stretch my legs out and cross them. "Okay." Confusion rings in my tone.

He lifts his gaze to mine. "It has to do with the society."

That reduces my confusion. "They're hazing her—that's what the message on the door was about." I had my suspicions already, but I also questioned if it was for Lily.

She's been bullied in the past, and we're all worried it'll carry on into this school, even though we're adults now. But people can be ruthless, and Lily became an easy target after that incident in high school, one that I only have the vague details of since she refuses to tell anyone all the specifics.

I've tried, many times.

"It's more than just hazing, brother." He flicks an invisible piece of lint off his shirt. "You know Eli's one of the leaders this year, right?" he asks, and I nod. "Well, he's shown an extra amount of interest in her. In fact, he's been relentlessly asking me questions about her because, apparently, word got out that we know each other. Although, I feel like that's a stretch. Still, he's been asking a lot about her, and it's just odd. I know Maddy is different from us in many ways, which could be behind his interest, but it doesn't feel that way ... Something is off. I just don't know what."

"Wait ... was he the one who grabbed her at the party?" Anger bites at my veins at the idea.

"I'm not sure, honestly. No one's mentioned it, but they also don't tell me everything, either."

"Maybe you should just leave the society. That way, they can't ask you questions. I don't know why you accepted the invitation when we both vowed never to join it." Bitterness lingers in my veins even now as I think about how Finn betrayed me and joined behind my back. He never explained why, either. Just said he had to.

While Finn and I usually have twin telepathy, it's been broken for the last couple of years, ever since our father had the affair, resulting in the divorce, a new stepmother, and the dissolving of our friendship with Noah.

"I can't." Finn sweeps a strand of his hair out of his eyes and sits back without elaborating, avoiding just like he always does. "What I can do is try to figure out what the society's interest in Maddy is. I just have to be careful."

"You sure you want to do that? You know there are a ton of risks if you get caught."

"You want me to just leave it and let the girl you've been obsessing about since we were in jail deal with it on her own?" he challenges, his brow curving upward. "Because she may be street smart, and even book smart, but Royal Society smart is something I don't believe she's ever had to deal with. They'll eat her alive—you know they will."

He's right, and while I wish I didn't care, I do.

"Fine, but be careful," I tell Finn. "And I don't think we should tell her anything until we know what's going on."

"We can try," Finn stresses, "but she's already been asking me a ton of questions about the society. I guess she's been researching online for some reason. Plus, she almost saw the secret entrance to the tunnel in the library."

That baffles the hell out of me. "What?"

"She saw me and Eli talking, and Lily told her that Eli bullied her, so Maddy thought it was weird that I was talking to him, and so Lily and her decided to follow me. They didn't see exactly where the entrance is, but Maddy saw me go into the library and that I didn't come out, so she's suspicious." He scratches his head. "Hopefully, she'll let it go, because if they find out she's looking into them, they might target her even harder."

"I still want to know why they're targeting her." I rub my hand across my forehead, feeling a headache coming on.

"We'll look into it," he assures me. "Until then, we'll keep an eye on her."

I nod in agreement.

We need to get answers before something worse than a message on the door happens to Maddy.

TWENTY-ONE
MADDISON

The shower is bigger than my bedroom at my house and has more showerheads than I'd ever think one person could need. The water is so warm too and remains that way the entire time. It's something I'm unused to so I end up staying in there for longer than I probably should.

By the time I climb out, my fingers are prune-y.

Once I dry off, I endeavor into Lily's closet to find something to wear. I feel so uncomfortable sifting through her clothes, so I make it quick, settling on the least expensive-looking outfit I can find—a loose pair of pants made with the softest material I've ever felt and a long-sleeve shirt that matches. As I'm pulling them on, I glance around her room, trying to imagine what it was like growing up in a place like this.

But as I'm taking everything in, my gaze zeroes in on a specific item.

On top of a vanity is a massive gold-trimmed jewelry box

with hooks on the top where necklaces are dangling. I move over to it and examine what's captured my attention—a necklace shaped like a crown that almost resembles the one my aunt Ellie gave me. The only difference is that Lily's is less scratched up and has a red diamond in it.

I turn it over and Lily's name has been engraved into the metal. Mine might have had an engraving on it one point, but it's too banged up now for it to be legible.

I'm so confused. How did my aunt get a necklace that resembles one that a royal owns?

Maybe she got it from a pawnshop? Still, it'd be expensive.

Perhaps it's some sort of counterfeit?

I decide to ask River about it, but as I'm exiting the bedroom, I smack into Finn with so much force that I hit my head on his chin and his teeth clank together.

"Jesus," Finn mutters, his tone laced with pain.

"Sorry," I quickly apologize, noting he smells good now, like freshly fallen rain with a splash of cologne. I hate that I notice that, and also how pretty he is.. "I didn't see you."

"Clearly." He's rubbing his jaw as I step back from him. His blonde hair is damp from the shower he must've taken and he's changed his clothes. "You good, though? You seemed in a hurry."

"Actually, I was." I point over my shoulder at Lily's room. "Can I ask you a question about something I found in there?"

He nods, a crease forming between his brows. "Um, sure."

He follows me to the jewelry box.

I touch the crown necklace. "Do you know where Lily got this?"

He slants forward to get a better look, giving me another good whiff of his wonderful scent. "Yeah, that's a coronation necklace. Royal girls are each given one when they're introduced to society. There's like this big ball and stuff. And I think the diamond color represents the family name, if I'm remembering correctly." He pauses, assessing me. "Why?"

I shrug, even more perplexed. "Because I have one."

I half expect him to be like *so*, but surprise flashes across his face. "What? How did you get it?"

"My aunt gave it to me when I was a kid," I explain. "But mine has a black diamond."

"Black... I don't think I've ever seen a black one."

"Hmm... Maybe mine's just counterfeit then." Because how else would my aunt have gotten it?

He nods, but a trace of uneasiness resides in his expression.

"What're you thinking?" I wonder suspiciously.

"Nothing." He shakes his nervousness away, suddenly appearing indifferent. "We should go check the cameras and see if the north-siders have left yet. I'd like to get back to the academy sooner rather than later."

With that he walks away, leaving it at that.

But I'm not about to. Not with everything strange going on. I want answers, and I will get them, even if it means playing Finn's royal game of truths and lies.

TWENTY-TWO
RIVER

I don't know where Maddy or Finn are, so I get to look for them. I'll admit, a part of me is worried they're hooking up. I don't think Maddy is like that, but Finn is. Although, since he believes I like Maddy, I doubt he'd do anything with her.

When I leave the living room area, I wander down the hallway and spot Finn ducking into his room. I follow him.

"What're you doing?" I ask.

"Shut the door," he hisses as he pulls out his phone.

I do as he instructs and shut the door before walking over to him and glancing at his screen.

He has the royal family archives app. open, and he's typing in his login information.

"Dude, what're you doing?" I ask perplexedly.

"Just give me a second," he replies as he searches through records until finally landing a list of diamonds that belong to each family.

He scrolls through that and stops on a photo of a black one. It's linked to a family name I don't recognize—the Everfords.

"Look at this." He points to the screen.

As I read the first few lines, I realize why I haven't heard of them.

Because their family name and bloodline ceased to exist and haven't since the 1970s.

"Okay... why am I reading this?" I glance at him, so damn confused.

He looks at me. "Maddy just told me, after she saw Lily's necklace, that she has one that looks just like this." He taps the screen.

"What?" Shock whips through. "How?"

"I have no clue." He closes the app. on his phone and sinks onto the bed. "I thought it could be counterfeit, but those are rare and usually they pulled from the market pretty quickly. My next guess was a pawn shop, but again, if a necklace ended up at a place like that, it'd be pricey."

"Where did Maddy get the necklace?" I wonder as I take a seat beside him.

"She said her aunt gave it to her." He pauses. "I might be overreacting, but with the society targeting her..." He blows out a breath. "It's weird, right?"

I nod in agreement, then dig out my phone to find more information about this necklace, and family name the diamond belongs to. But there's not much more than what I just read, and it leaves me confused.

Why would Maddy have a necklace belonging to a family that ceases to exist? Jewelry belonging to a dead royal name would likely be auctioned off for an extremely high price.

And again, I can't stop thinking about how the society has shown so much interest in Maddy. With so much uncertainty surrounding her, she's hugely at risk.

I need a foolproof plan to keep Maddy out of the society's eye.

"Is there any way I can protect her from the society?" I wonder as I rake my fingers through my hair. "There's rules, right?" I ask, and Finn nods. "Well, isn't there a loophole in one of them that could protect her?

I can tell by his expression that there is, and he finds it mildly amusing.

I sigh heavily. "Just tell me what it is."

The corners of his lips tug upward. "You could join the society and then date her."

I blink at him. "What?"

"There's a rule that states the society can't target or haze members girlfriends or boyfriends." He shrugs. "So I guess it all depends on how much you like this girl, because I know you hate the society, and you've spent your entire life refusing to date anyone."

My stomach plummets. I have no desire to join, but can I just let Maddy fend for herself? She already seems like she has so many problems.

The real question is: why am I obsessed with this girl? From the moment I laid eyes on her in jail, I've wanted to protect her, no matter what the cost.

And I have a feeling that I'm about to do it again.

ABOUT THE AUTHOR

Jessica Sorensen is a *New York Times* and *USA Today* bestselling author who lives in the snowy mountains of Wyoming. When she's not writing, she spends her time reading and hanging out with her family.

For more info:

Facebook: Jessica.Sorensen.Author

Facebook group: Sorensen's Stars

Instagram: jessica_sorensenauthor

jessicasorensen.com

<u>The Royal Academy:</u>

The Royal Academy

The Royal Secret

The Royal Promise (coming soon)

<u>Forget Me Not:</u>

Forget Me Not

Untitled (coming soon)

<u>The Honeyton Mysteries:</u>

Chasing Hadley

Untitled (coming soon)

<u>The Sunnyvale Mysteries:</u>

The Year I Became Isabella Anders

The Year of Falling in Love

The Year of Second Chances

<u>Standalones:</u>

Rules of Willow & Beck

Confessions of Luna & Grey

The Illusion of Annabella

The Forgotten Girl

Breathing Lies

The Opposite of Ordinary

<u>Lexi Ashford Series:</u>

The Diary of Lexi Ashford

The Diary of Lexi Ashford: The Agreement

Untitled (coming soon)

<u>The Unraveling Mysteries Series:</u>

Unraveling You

Raveling You

Awakening You

Inspiring You

<u>Shadow Cove Series:</u>

What Lies in the Darkness

Untitled (coming soon)

<u>The Coincidence Series:</u>

The Coincidence of Callie and Kayden

The Redemption of Callie and Kayden

The Destiny of Violet and Luke

The Probability of Violet and Luke

The Certainty of Violet and Luke

The Resolution of Callie and Kayden

Seth & Greyson

The Secret Series:

The Prelude of Ella and Micha

The Secret of Ella and Micha

The Forever of Ella and Micha

The Temptation of Lila and Ethan

The Ever After of Ella and Micha

Lila and Ethan: Forever and Always

Ella and Micha: Infinitely and Always

Breaking Nova Series:

Breaking Nova

Saving Quinton

Delilah: The Making of Red

Nova and Quinton: No Regrets

Tristan: Finding Hope

Wreck Me

Ruin me

Unbeautiful Series:

Unbeautiful

Untamed

<u>**Tangled Realms:**</u>

Forever Violet (standalone)

Untitled (coming soon)

<u>**Harlynn's Mystery Investigations:**</u>

Sugar Cookies & Zombie Secrets

Untitled (coming soon)

<u>**Mystic Willow Bay Mysteries Series:**</u>

The Secret Life of a Witch

Broken Magic

Stolen Magic (coming soon)

<u>**Enchanted Chaos Series:**</u>

Enchanted Chaos (standalone)

Untitled (coming soon)

<u>**Capturing Magic:**</u>

Chasing Wishes

Untitled (coming soon)

<u>**My Cursed Superhero Life:**</u>

Grim

Untitled (coming soon)

<u>**Guardian Academy Series:**</u>

Entranced

Entangled

Untitled (coming soon)

<u>Monster Academy for the Magical:</u>

Monster Academy for the Magical

Monster Academy for the Magical: Hidden Magic

Monster Academy for the Magical: The Monster Clique (coming soon)

<u>The Shattered Promises Series:</u>

Shattered Promises

Fractured Souls

Unbroken

Broken Visions

Scattered Ashes

<u>The Fallen Star Series:</u>

The Fallen Star

The Underworld

The Vision

The Promise

The Lost Soul

The Evanescence

<u>The Darkness Falls Series:</u>

Darkness Falls

Darkness Breaks

Darkness Fades

<u>The Death Collectors Series (NA and YA):</u>

Ember X and Ember

Cinder X and Cinder

Spark X and Spark

www.ingramcontent.com/pod-product-compliance
Lightning Source LLC
Chambersburg PA
CBHW050612190726
48283CB00007B/2381